His Name Was Death

T0268655

Rafael Bernal

HIS NAME
WAS DEATH

translated by Kit Schluter

A NEW DIRECTIONS
PAPERBOOK ORIGINAL

Copyright © 1947 by Rafael Bernal
Copyright © 2020 by Latin American Rights Agency, Groupo Planeta
Translation copyright © 2021 by Kit Schluter
Introduction copyright © 2021 by Yuri Herrera

Published by arrangement with Editorial Planeta Mexicana and Grupo Planeta
Originally published in 1947 as *Su nombre era muerte*

All rights reserved.
Except for brief passages quoted in a newspaper, magazine, radio, television,
or website review, no part of this book may be reproduced in any form or
by any means, electronic or mechanical, including photocopying and recording,
or by any information storage and retrieval system, without permission
in writing from the Publisher.

Manufactured in the United States of America
First published as a New Directions Paperbook Original (NDP1517) in 2021.
Design by Erik Rieselbach

Library of Congress Cataloging-in-Publication Data
Names: Bernal, Rafael, 1915–1972, author. | Schluter, Kit, translator.
Title: His name was death / Rafael Bernal ; translated by Kit Schluter.
Other titles: Su nombre era muerte. English
Description: First edition. |
New York : New Directions Publishing Corporation, 2021.
Identifiers: LCCN 2021037306 | ISBN 9780811230834 (paperback) |
ISBN 9780811230841 (ebook)
Subjects: LCGFT: Novels.
Classification: LCC PQ7297.B38 S813 2021 | DDC 863/.64—dc23
LC record available at https://lccn.loc.gov/2021037306

4 6 8 10 9 7 5

New Directions Books are published for James Laughlin
by New Directions Publishing Corporation
80 Eighth Avenue, New York 10011

And I looked, and behold a pale horse: and his name that sat on him was Death, and Hell followed with him. And power was given unto them over the fourth part of the earth, to kill MAN with sword, and with hunger, and with death, and with beasts of the earth.

APOCALYPSE 6:8

Introduction

Rife with concerns so strikingly central to our own zeitgeist, *His Name Was Death* was written at a time when the human responsibility for destroying the environment and the possibility of other species' having consciousness were topics of marginal interest at best.

The author wasn't trying to be ahead of his times or "experimental"—and yet, in this 1940s science fiction novel, the encounter between alien civilizations happens thanks to linguistics, not spaceships. Rafael Bernal was simply a writer who truly contained multitudes, and in his work, as in his life, he kept reinventing himself.

Bernal was born in 1915, during the Revolution, and died in 1972, when the revolutionary project was well past its zenith and starting to decay. His work is infused with criticism of the official national history, from the violence which destroyed the old order to the means by which the new state stabilized the country. Chief among what he saw as unforgivable acts was the way the State treated the Catholic Church and its parishioners, especially after the bloody episode known as Guerra Cristera, a war waged between 1926 and 1929. It began as a clash of two profoundly authoritarian forces: on one side, an anticlerical group within the triumphant revolutionaries; on the other, a radicalized Catholic Church that opposed certain articles of the 1917 Constitution, especially those concerning secular education. What started as a rhetorical confrontation soon became an armed, bloody conflict: by its close, a quarter million people had been killed. The

Guerra Cristera only ended when both sides understood that in the short term no military resolution was possible, and they negotiated in secret. This mode of conflict resolution highlights important workings of the ancien régime, with its preferred strategy for deactivating clashes: the secret agreements, the ambiguous promises, the domestication of political opponents.

Bernal was not a soldier in that war, but he was on the losing side in terms of his ideological inclinations, in a faction which—unlike other parties on the losing side of the Guerra Cristera that negotiated with the government or became part of PAN, the other right-wing party—tried to forward an ultra-Catholic, fiercely anticommunist agenda through Synarchism. As a young man, Bernal was a militant in the Synarchist Fuerza Popular Party, a populist, grassroots movement that worked with peasants and social organizations and which took its inspiration from the fascist movements on the rise in Europe, but lacking power and a wide social base, never had any real influence in national politics. After a short period he walked away from Synarchism (which, eventually, as with most opposition parties of the time, was deactivated). Bernal, after earning his bachelor's degree at Loyola in Montreal and then his doctorate in literature from the University of Fribourg in Switzerland, held a variety of cultural positions. (He also studied at the Colegio Francés de San Borja in Peru and at the Instituto de Ciencias y Letras in Mexico City.) He was a journalist stationed in Paris during the Second World War, worked in early Mexican TV, founded a publishing house that specialized in poetry, taught history at various colleges, and later in life became a diplomat. He served in Honduras, the Philippines, Peru, and Switzerland (where he died), representing a regime that, in his literary works, deserved nothing but scorn.

Just as he was a man of many parts in life, Bernal felt free in his literary works to roam about among genres: he wrote short stories and plays refuting triumphalist versions of post-Independence

Mexican history; he also wrote stories about seamen and detective novels. In *The Strange Case of Aloysius Hands, Death in the Tomb*, and *Of Natural Death*, Bernal employed the classic tropes of the detective novel, with its central crime that must be solved by deductive skills. Then he abandoned this mold and wrote his most celebrated work. Now hailed as the first Mexican noir, this novel is, among other things, a codification of his era's political practices and a denunciation of the Manichaeism of the Cold War: *The Mongolian Conspiracy*.

Here, in *His Name Was Death*, in a very nineteenth-century ideological key, Bernal writes about the dichotomy between civilization and barbarism, placing his plot in Chiapas, where he had lived, and it is to this period that *His Name Was Death* belongs. This is the story of a man who hates. Throughout the novel we meet several objects of his hatred, but in reality he hates humanity. More than that, it is hate itself that nourishes him and leads him away from civilization and into the jungle, where a cosmic encounter takes place between this human and another species— one that, like humanity, confidently knows itself to be the owner of the universe.

He learns the language of that other species, the mosquitoes, and it turns out they are not only rational but terrifyingly rational. They have detailed records of what they have said and done in the last half a million years; they are rigid, merciless, and totalitarian. Mosquito society is organized in inflexible castes, at the top of which is the Supreme Council, a closed elite that have already thought everything that is to be thought, hence they do nothing but watch to see that the order is respected, since their society is just, peaceful, perfect. It is with these insects that the protagonist with no name is going to strike a deal.

Among the many things that make this story compelling is that *His Name Was Death* is full of violent hesitation and contradictions. A sort of libertarian manifesto, it denounces allegorically the worst nightmares of the twentieth century: the devaluation of the individual, the sacrifice of millions for an ideology, the blind obedience of the masses. At the same time, it is a novel that still sees the American continent, especially the jungle, through a colonialist lens: the Lacandon Indians that the protagonist finds in the jungle see him, bearded and white, as a god; and the best thing he thinks he can do is to bring them "civilization."

It is telling that what breaks up the alliance of the hero with the mosquitoes is not their totalitarianism but that they negate the existence of God, and God, he contends, is the true origin of freedom, the true evidence of the dignity of all life. Battles, murder, lust, and rebellion ensue.

Predictably, Bernal was sidelined in a cultural field dominated by a handful of patriarchs who defined what should be treasured as "truly" Mexican and what should be forgotten. He was forgotten. For a while. Then he was rescued the way every writer wishes to be rescued, by readers hanging on to his books generation after generation, until they get a new life.

His Name Was Death, by the way, is also a book about the power of writing. Again and again the protagonist repeats that he is writing his diary not only to warn humanity of the dangers he has known, but to achieve immortality. That poor guy is still a guy with no name, if not death. Rafael Bernal, though, even if he passed away in 1972, is still among us.

YURI HERRERA

His Name Was Death

I

Perhaps all my work will come to nothing and it's too late to start these memoirs; death has me surrounded, and I don't know how much time I have left. I see now that I should have started writing them before, when I still wielded power over death itself, but I will write my chronicle for mankind now, for the good of the human race, and back when I still had the time to write I wouldn't have wanted to: I didn't consider myself a member of such a ridiculous organization. No, I saw in myself a superior being—a hostile, offended soul, filled with the desire for revenge, and well-possessed of the power to take it.

Now, forsaken by everything that had given me my immense power, I feel once more like a human being, a man like any other, terrified by the annihilation looming before me and full of a foolish longing for immortality, for life beyond this petty clay. And so I write these memoirs, fully aware that in the brief stint of life I have left they'll be worthless to me. I only hope, by way of these pages, to survive my death in the memory of humankind, whom I now wish to serve.

In all honesty, I have never done humans any harm; I have only offended them with my thoughts and passions, and if I ever did do them wrong, it was only by omission—I refused them the greatest gift any man could ever possibly have given. For, you see, I could have become something of a "Super Pasteur," but my hatred, which I now recognize as foolish, and my lust for power lured me down other paths. It's true, mankind never did anything whatsoever for me, and even now, with death inescapably looming, I still can't say if what I did was right or wrong. I have no regrets. But when the moment came for me to decide between goodness and my own ambitions, I felt myself spurred on by my hatred of society, by the anxiety I carried inside, by my memories of all the bitterness, all the selfishness I had seen and been subjected to. And even now, with death so close at hand, stripped of my power and feeling myself human once more, I refuse to say that I love mankind. In all my past experience, I find no reason for loving humanity, however much I may belong to it and constitute a part of its world. I sit here now—awaiting death under wretched lamplight, with the jungle shivering and howling outside my door—and I start my memoirs, fully aware I am doing so as much out of an imperious desire to immortalize myself in the memory of the very people I have always hated as out of any innate sense of human solidarity.

If my only interest were mankind's benefit, I would tell my story plainly, point out the danger bearing down on the human race, suggest a solution, and mention nothing of my personal life. But I am not writing this out of kindness: I am writing it because I want to be known—known and never forgotten. I am writing so my name, the very one on the first page of this book, will survive so long as there is a world. The certainty that I will live on in my work calms this awful fear creeping into me while I await my death.

The part of my life of any importance whatsoever has been brief: only four years, from my forty-fifth to my forty-ninth year, the year in which I find myself now. Everything that came before was no more than a prelude to bitterness: the bitterness that is the beating heart of these four important years, the motivation of all my actions. But I don't want to talk about what came before. On the cover of this notebook I have already scrawled my name and nationality. Leave it to the historians—they can try to piece my story back together until they themselves have gotten lost in the

4

jungle's caves. Suffice it to say that, in my first forty-four years, I reaped nothing but bitterness—bitterness and hatred.

The cruelty of mankind—and the disgust my contact with it provoked—hurled me from the great cities to the margins of civilization, until I found myself in Chiapas. For a time I lived with the Chamula people by the limpid banks of the Grijalva; there, I dwelled in quiet solitude, interrupted only now and then by human cruelty. But my spirit was seeking an ever deeper solitude, and every time I suffered contact with civilization was unbearable torture. With each word they spoke to me, the past welled up again, filling my soul with a silent anxiety that clutched at my throat; and I longed to hurt, to kill, to inflict irreparable damage. But the absurd necessity of making a living forced me to deal with people, and now, as I remember those dealings, I loathe them more than ever. Whenever I made a little money, I did anything possible to forget, and I would drink to the point of falling facedown in the street, where nobody was compassionate enough to help me back to my feet. In the eyes of the world I was a despicable boozehound, the object of brain-dead laughter, but I considered myself more the victim than the offender—if I was a drunk, it was the world's fault.

In search of a more complete solitude, I walked across the Sierra until I reached the banks of the Usumacinta in San Quintín, that site of hatred and death, where parched, infirm, rotten men seek in the jungle the precious wood and chicle that they haul off to cities just as sick and corrupt: the souls of such men are rotten to the core, and wherever they go, they never find anything more than what they already carry within.

There I found a truer jungle and ventured deep into its swarming, gnarled vegetation, floating up its silty channels in my lonesome canoe, in search of some way to make a living that would allow me to achieve total solitude, and save me any further hideous contact with "civilized" humans. And there I came to know the destructive jungle, the hostile jungle, the jungle that perspires death; and yet it was still better than the cities, somehow gentler, more benign. The jungle: misfortune's cloak and bitter hatred's blind—the blessed jungle. Whoever would live inside her can find peace, so long as he submits to her laws and doesn't mind being a lowly admirer of such magnificence, so long as he doesn't mind setting aside his human pride and becoming no more than an unwelcome guest, a fledgling stripped of his rights, content to vegetate in the shadows of the jungle's goodwill.

And so I lived by the banks of the slothful Usumacinta, in a wretched palm-leaf hut, with no belongings save a hammock, a rifle, and a handful of old books gnawed away by humidity and time. Sometimes I made it out to the towns to sell my jaguar pelts and heron feathers, to buy rifle cartridges and the jugs of liquor I would carry home along some riverbed to my hut, where I could devote myself entirely to drinking and forget my lamentable condition as a human. Life, like that, felt tolerable. My only torment was the mosquitoes—by night they gorged themselves on my blood and, by day, stalked me until I was forced to flee the shadows of the trees and make for the beaches, where the sun, falling vertically upon my back, burned with the crack of a gargantuan whip from the great, open skies. My head, all through the eternal, insomniac nights, pounded with the lines of some poet—I don't know which—who must have also suffered such unremitting torments, a poet well-versed in the jungle's bitterness, aware of his own terror, his own lethargic death:

> Who am I to say how the jungle learned
> the art of weeping?
> I'd heard tell of some such sorrow,
> of machetes turning soft
> before the fertile murder of the earth,
> and I lingered up, all the starless night
> sprawling by the riverside,
> under the sound-awning of mosquitoes.

Maybe death would have been the best solution. I remember one day, as I lay there on the streets of Tumbalá, trying to wake up from a night of drinking, a man nudged me with his foot and said:

"The way you're living, you'd be better off dead."

The phrase got stuck in my head: it became a part of me, taking me by surprise at night whenever the mosquitoes were tormenting me and I didn't have on hand the soothing balm of alcohol. Many times I approached the riverbank, meditating on how simple it would have been to wade into the water until the current carried me away in its chilly arms. But the slapping tail of some caiman, which perhaps had intuited my thoughts, gave me such a fright that I found myself streaking back to the safety of my hammock, where the dawn found me sobbing. On other occasions I meditated on the brevity of a gunshot, but the fear, the terrible fear of not existing, of possibly never having existed at all, restrained my finger, which lay then upon my rifle's trigger.

Throughout all the tragedies—of which I mustn't speak—and throughout all my days of heavy drinking, hatred, and bitterness, I have been subject to this terrible desire to exist, which at present drives me to take up this pen to entrust my secrets to the world. As a boy, I first dreamt of winning glory on the battlefield, and my childhood reveries oozed with heroism. Later I longed to make my name in the world of letters, but every door was slammed in my face. Even so, I am certain I harbor the spirit of a man capable of writing marvelous things. It's strange that now, after so many years, after so much tragedy and disaster, after such glory and power, here, by the muddy banks of the Metasboc, with death nipping at my heels—"with one foot already in the stirrup," I might say along with Cervantes—I am once again entrusting my immortality to my pen.

For five years I lived the hunter's life, at the end of which time I had lost even the desire to leave the jungle, not because I liked it, not because I had grown accustomed to its obscure way of life, not even because I had resigned myself to this lethargic death, but because liquor and anxiety, jungle fever and moral poverty had stripped me of the strength required for any desire or action at all.

I wandered for five years through the Usumacinta jungle, penetrating deep into the heart of the bush, reaching places unknown to other white men. From there I pushed beyond the mysterious Metasboc and on to the huts of the Petén Basin, only then to return to the towns with my load of pelts, feathers, and misery.

From time to time I would build my shelter beside the caribal, or tribal village, of some group or other of miserable Lacandon, a people forgotten deep in the heart of the jungle, who know nothing of our civilization beyond its murderous liquor and the endless predations of the colonizers. It was beside one such caribal that I met Yellow Bird and Nocturnal Raccoon, two venerable tribal chiefs, high priests of I don't know which forgotten gods, and the only true friends I've ever had.

Once I had picked up the Lacandon's language, I found them easy to get along with, and I held them in much higher esteem than I did any men of my own race. They live in a semibarbaric state agreeable to someone who wants to be alone but needs the occasional helping hand. Little by little I stopped appearing in the towns and performed all my trades with the Lacandon, mostly with Yellow Bird's tribe, which consisted of nine men and five coveted women, the mothers of eleven dirty, potbellied children. During the last three of those five nomadic years of little importance, my hut never moved from its place near their caribal. I gave them meat from the animals I hunted and protected them from the claws of jaguars and white traders. They, in return, gave me a bit of corn or yucca, and their silent friendship.

It's useless now to describe those five years I spent wandering between jungle paths and fetid huts. They are bound to be lost along with my former years, of no importance whatsoever. But time is short and better spent writing down the things that matter.

II

The story I'm going to tell begins about four years ago, in the rainy season when the earth finds itself flooded, when all the streams flow into one another and the jungle turns into one great impassable swamp. I was living in a small clearing by the reddish waters of the Lacantún River, some two hundred yards from Yellow Bird's land. For more than two months I'd been suffering from constant, recurrent shivering fits. I never left my hut, but spent my days dozing in my hammock and my nights killing mosquitoes with my bare hands and piling up their corpses on the crate I had set up as my table. There's a certain pleasure in killing a mosquito with your bare hands, crushing its body between your sweaty palms, taking it in your fingers to set it down on a pile of other dead ones in a clay pot, and then rejoicing over the spectacle the following morning.

One of the women there was something of a shaman; they called her Black Ant. She often took care of me when I was sick, giving me the corn she had cooked for me and bringing me water. Seeing the pot full of these dead mosquitoes every morning, she became strangely determined to believe that I too was a shaman, cooking up medicine with their corpses. I never could convince her that it was only a harmless pastime, inspired by my soul's implacable hatred for their inane buzzing. Despite my protests, she forged right ahead with her belief and told her whole tribe, who all quickly looked upon me with a certain amount of fear, and much greater respect.

Many of them started coming to me in search of medicine for their fevers, and I gave them a bit of quinine, which brought them relief. This increased my renown but diminished Black Ant's, so, fearing her wrath, and desiring above all to keep the peace, I joined forces with her. Whenever the sick came to me, I suggested they go see their own medicine woman (all the while providing her with white powders she mixed together with all sorts of junk—water-spider bellies and other such things—and doled out to the sick, singing amid fragrant clouds of incense smoke). I still believe Black Ant is one of the most intelligent women I've ever met. She has already buried three husbands, and now, at sixty, is married to a twenty-year-old who considers himself lucky to be the husband of such an illustrious witch.

Meanwhile, the mosquitoes continued to torment me in my hut. I had long since grown numb to their bites, but their constant buzzing around my head still drove me mad, filling me with such hatred and anger that I came to despise the mosquitoes as much as I despised mankind.

In my youth I had been a bit studious, and now, in the forced repose of the rainy season, with little alcohol to help pass my time, I devoted myself to the study of mosquitoes: soon I could differentiate between over a hundred types of the genus *Anopheles*.

I became completely absorbed by my studies and began to delve into the question of the mosquitoes' social organization. One thing I noticed that didn't make any sense to me at first was that so many more mosquitoes appear during the season when a great deal of ripe fruit is hanging on the trees, because I had gathered that their gestation, from the moment the female lays her little eggs in a puddle until the offspring is able to fly out of its cocoon, takes about three weeks—so if the females laid more eggs when there were enough fruit in the trees to survive, as might be expected, the young would be born three weeks later and the population increase would be noticed then. Given that their increase took place at the exact same time as the fruits', however, I figured they must have had a brain capable of foresight, since the females were laying their eggs ahead of time, such that the young would be born when an ample food supply was assured. Later on I discovered the reasons for all of this, but in the beginning I was merely grasping at straws, assuming there must be *some* kind of organization. I never could have imagined, though, just how complete and marvelous an organization it truly was.

I also observed that only two or three mosquitoes would fly into my hut at first, but once they'd bitten me, many more would filter in before long. This led me to think that they had some sort of communication system, which they used to alert each other whenever they had successfully drawn blood from any ad hoc creature. Because the females are the ones who bite and suck blood, my hut was often full of them, while the males only occasionally appeared. Yet if I left a slice of fruit out on the table, several males would come sucking at its sweetness, especially if it was ripe mango or sapodilla. Still, the question was, if they did communicate, how did it work? Maybe they communicated via minuscule waves emitted by their antennae, like ants and certain other insects, or maybe their constant buzzing, in fact, served as a language. But something else troubled me, as well: if they could communicate with each other, why did they still keep coming after me, even though I killed so many of them night after night, instead of attacking some other animal, a deer, for example, which would have made for easier prey? Instead, they attacked me and they attacked the toads, which also killed them mercilessly—and gobbled them up.

As I said before, the bites didn't bother me anymore, and I was no longer afraid of fever, my steadfast companion. But what still drove me to despair was that constant buzzing, that coming and going over my head, that exasperating trail of sound. One day I decided that this buzzing *must* be their system of communication.

I was already fully convinced they could communicate just as well as humans did using words, and perhaps with even greater ease. With this idea in mind, I began to study their buzzes and realized they weren't all the same—no, there were longer ones, higher-pitched ones, deeper ones, some that were intermittent while others were constant—and then I understood it wasn't simply that each mosquito had a different tone of voice, but that each insect could produce a variety of tones. In the beginning I believed the buzzes were like telegraph signals, each pulse denoting a letter or a word, perhaps even a complete idea. But if that had been the case, surely the buzzes would have all been alike in pitch, since the durations of the pulses and pauses alone would have been the keys to understanding the message being buzzed.

My observations on the mosquitoes, their life, and their possible language kept my mind off my sadness throughout the whole rainy season those four years ago. I wasn't afraid of the night, as I had been before; rather, I longed for it to come, so I could stay awake, studying the buzzes and holding them in my memory, trying to fully understand them before forming my hypotheses.

But bitterness suddenly rushed back into me, and I fell prey to desperation. I don't know which of the soul's obscure paths despair took to reach my throat, just as in earlier times. One night I needed the consolation of liquor, needed it like never before—I needed alcohol with an insane, irrepressible thirst. I screamed alone in my hut, damning everything, damning the disgrace of mankind and my beloved jungle, damning the lazy rivers, as dirty as my life. Unable to control myself, I snuck into Yellow Bird's home and stole off with the guardian liquor; I hid myself away on a beach and I drank, drank until I was thrashing in the sand, screaming out my hatred and despair, while all around me the magnanimous jungle held its silence, aghast at the pettiness of man.

The following morning, shame and loathing forced me to quit my hut and withdraw deep into the jungle, far from all human contact, where I could drink alone, free of the silent reproach of my friends the Lacandon.

I spent two months back in the hell of liquor. Hidden away in the belly of the jungle, I drank and cursed mankind for casting me down into such an abyss. Sometimes I didn't eat for entire days, but spent them sprawled out on some beach drinking and feeling hatred, always feeling hatred. I knew this path could lead only to death, but I longed for death, redemptive death, that repose free of hatred, free of bitterness. I don't know when I lost consciousness. I sank into the alcoholic mist and the jungle took me into its arms like a good mother—or a dangerous lover. Nor do I know for how long I was unconscious, dead to everything, everything but the fire I carried within. I may have wandered along the rivers and streams; the Lacandon say I was shooting my gun into the air and that my roaring laughter, my sobbing, and my screams tore out from the deepest ends of the paths. They tell me that I was stalking through the jungle without a machete, clearing my way forward with my bare hands, my teeth, with an endless longing to arrive somewhere, anywhere—to break, to destroy. The jungle cackled around me, cackled at my pettiness, at the poverty of this sorry, rotten soul of mine that I was dragging along waterways just as rotten. I don't know how long my delirium lasted, I don't remember any of my actions, or the words I screamed, the bitter words surging up inside me.

When I awoke, the morning was bright. I was stretched out in my hammock, hurting in body and soul. Yellow Bird leaned down over me and said:

"White man, my friend and friend of the tribe: the devil who hides himself in alcohol has now, by the grace of Black Ant, departed from you. We have summoned the four good Balams and the Cross of your race: we have offered up fresh honey in sacrifice, and behold how the spirits have heard our call and driven away the demons who tormented you for so long. The four good winds have blown upon your face, and you have been cleansed. Do not think we bear you any ill will. Rather, we would ask you to stay and live among us forever, for we enjoy your company; you know how to drive away the devils of fever and chills, and the good spirits often speak through your mouth. Stay with us, for you are like the owl, who knows so much."

The demons of bitterness and desperation truly had left me, and I chose to stay near Yellow Bird's encampment. I think that brutal crisis of hate-crazed delirium had purged my soul of all its bitterness. I no longer felt any hatred or anxiety: the knot that had seized my throat for so long had come loose, and I was left with nothing but a terrible laziness. Yellow Bird's words—the first words of praise and hope anyone had ever addressed to me—had soothed my soul. Finally someone believed in me, in my way of seeing things, and in the goodness of my person.

And so I surrendered to the sloth of the jungle, and throughout that entire dry season I never once shot my rifle by the streams, nor glimpsed the impotent caiman slapping its tail, nor any malicious jaguar lying in waiting. Yellow Bird and his people looked after me, and I advised them—advised them always in what I believed would be for their good—guided by my hatred for the men of my race.

III

As soon as my delirium passed, I resumed my studies of the mosquitoes, trying to recall everything I had observed before, and writing down my ideas for the first time. I was still taken with the theory that the mosquitoes have some system of communication based on their buzzing, which to human ears seems so irritating and pointless.

To imagine this meant to imagine that mosquitoes are possessed of a higher intelligence and a societal organization likely similar to that of ants and termites, only much ampler, not being relegated to ridiculous holes in the ground or tree trunks. If such an organization did exist, it must have been more perfect than the ants', even if it appeared less precise at first glance. But wishing to study mosquitoes and their society without first understanding their method of communication is like wishing to study a foreign country when one's met only a handful of its inhabitants and never been able to speak with them. First of all, I had to learn Mosquil—which was the name I gave to their language—in order to understand the countless aspects of their lives and customs I didn't understand. For example, if they really were intelligent, why did they spend their nights trying to drink my blood when I killed so many of them? I kept careful statistics of the mosquitoes who successfully bit me and the ones I killed before they could, and by the end of one month I saw that, for every hundred mosquitoes who managed to suck my blood, only eleven made it out alive, and many more had also died before they could even bite me. In one month alone I killed three thousand six hundred forty-nine, of which only two thousand three hundred twenty-four had sucked my blood, which indicated that one thousand three hundred twenty-five had died before they could carry out their mission. I estimate, since I was unable to count them, that during that month my hut was host to more than fifteen thousand mosquitoes, of which only two hundred and fifty-seven were able to make it out alive after biting me. What was certain was that I had become extraordinarily skilled in the art of killing mosquitoes, and that any other man would have been able to kill only a small fraction of the ones I killed, but in any case, for an intelligent life form, as I now imagined the mosquitoes to be, the benefits from biting one man could not justify the casualties they incurred.

From this I deduced that mosquitoes suffered casualties in pursuit of their goal just as the general who must gain a position key to his victory makes sacrifices in order to win it, regardless of however many men might be necessary. At first I imagined that the mosquitoes were enslaved by, or somehow subject to, malarial germs, and that these agents were forcing the mosquitoes to bite humans in order to propagate themselves, regardless of their vehicles' deaths—much as the modern soldier doesn't think twice about sacrificing his armored car and whatever cargo it may be carrying in order to achieve his goal. And yet I wasn't convinced. I knew that some mosquitoes carried malaria while others didn't, but that they attacked regardless; so I couldn't conclude they were all slaves to the malarial parasite. Malaria was probably just one of the mosquitoes' many weapons, a particular feature of their warfare, like the artillery in human armies.

All these enigmas drove me on, sleepless and studious, certain that I would never be able to solve them until I came to understand the language. With this in mind, I dedicated myself body and soul to cataloging the various buzzes I heard at night, writing down the context of the noises that had been emitted and what

I imagined they might mean. In order to transcribe the buzzing, I developed a system to represent the pulses, their sharpness or depth, the lengths of the rests, and the musical notes in which they were produced. I quickly saw, regarding the notes, that mosquitoes use the semitones of the scale, such that each range contains twelve different sounds of varying pitch. In the beginning it was hard to tell them apart, but little by little I attuned my ear—and here the musical training I had received as a child proved extremely useful.

After several months of study I realized that each phrase was emitted in one of the four human vocal ranges, and that every phrase was emitted entirely within the same range, regardless of whether the next phrase or the previous one had been in another. For example: one mosquito might buzz momentarily, producing eight or ten pulses in the bass range, let's say, only to enter the tenor or baritone range (or, perhaps, although this was uncommon, the soprano range). Of course, the range of their sounds isn't identical to our own, but it does bear a strong resemblance, and this can be followed as a rule of thumb.

Once I had observed and confirmed the tonal consistency of each phrase, I decided not to theorize any further, but busied myself with gathering more information, faithfully transcribing the sounds I heard and the contexts of their emissions. I noticed a particular sound, the bass-voice E repeated twice with a short rest. It was repeated often at night and I realized that, as soon as one mosquito produced it, others always rushed over to her, from which I deduced it must serve as a summoning call. Then I observed that this same note in the baritone range had the contrary effect, and that the mosquitoes near the one producing it tended to retreat; it was generally buzzed while I was killing or trying to swat them. With this data, I ventured to formulate the theory that in Mosquil the range determines the mood of the verb, such that if "E, rest, E" in the bass range signified "Come!" then in the baritone range it necessarily meant, "Do not come!" One night, I left a wounded mosquito on my bed and noticed she was buzzing entirely in the high-pitched soprano range. Each of her phrases began with "E, rest, E," but no other mosquito paid her any mind, until a larger one landed beside her. The wounded mosquito, still using the very high-pitched soprano range, buzzed several notes, and the big one answered, "C, D, G, E, C, D," each note followed by a short rest, except the D and the G, and once he had finished buzzing he killed the smaller one, leaving her corpse behind on my rickety cot. I repeated the same experiment many times and observed that the wounded one always emitted the same sounds, but that the larger mosquito who then appeared, after listening to the wounded one, sometimes offered the same reply as the one from my first example, putting the one who had called to him out of her misery, but other times replied with a phrase in the tenor range, which the wounded one would then answer in the bass range. In the latter cases, other mosquitoes would arrive and carry her away without killing her.

From these and other observations, I deduced that Mosquil verbs uttered in the bass range are always declarative; in baritone range, negative; in tenor, interrogative; and in the very high-pitched soprano range, either imperative or exclamatory. I had also observed that the verb is always some compound of the note E, that when the verb is singular a natural note is employed, while plural verbs call for the sharp: thus, "I go" is "E-natural, rest, E-natural, bass," and "we go" is "E-sharp, rest, E-sharp, bass." In my annotation system, I numbered the dozen semitones from one to twelve, the four voice ranges "D" for bass, or deep, "T" for tenor, "B" for baritone, and "S" for soprano. I denoted rests with the letter "R" if they were short and "L" if they were long, and always placed the voice's range before each sentence. And so, the verb "I go" would be expressed as: "D 5 R 5." Keep in mind that the rests, in the case of the majority of mosquitoes, and particularly if they are speaking quickly, aren't true pauses, but merely brief intervals during which the voice is lowered but does not cease to buzz, which leads the untrained ear to hear it as an unbroken sound.

More and more excited by my studies, I quit drinking completely, as well as all trading and hunting. The Lacandon continued to support me, and they never dared interrupt me when they saw me busy with my notebooks, unless they considered it a matter of absolute urgency. One day Yellow Bird came to visit me. He watched my activities from afar for a while, before finally venturing to speak:

"Wise Owl," he said to me, "we have learned that the men of your race are approaching these riverbanks to seek the excellent wood of this jungle, and we the Lacandon have no interest in negotiating with them, so we have decided to ask your counsel on whether we should leave for the holy Metasboc, where no white man has ever set foot before, or stay behind to trade with them and receive their blankets, knives, and liquor. Speak, Wise Owl, for the entire tribe awaits your word and knows that your guidance is inspired by the good spirits you capture in your notebooks with strokes of dark ink."

Yellow Bird's way of talking, it seemed to me, was always a bit pompous: he gave me the impression he had read Fenimore Cooper's novels and that he was trying to imitate the way Indians speak in them. Though, when it came to questions or commands—or reproaches, above all—he forewent his normal eloquence and, peppering his mother tongue with Spanish, achieved phrases all the more expressive for it. In any event, his pomp always made me laugh just a bit whenever he spoke to me of serious matters. This time, I restrained my amusement and answered:

"I am grateful, Yellow Bird, for the trust you and your tribe have placed in both me and the spirits that guide me. You know your tribe is my family, that the men of my race are nothing to me and I nothing to them, so I will advise you with good words,

words I reserve exclusively for a brother. Let us begin our great march to the holy Metasboc without delay; let us flee the men of my race who, should they provide your tribe with liquor, will have enclosed evil spirits in that drink, and soon you will all be their slaves and peace will no longer prosper among your people."

I could tell that my words did not please him, since he had assumed I would try to stay behind and see the men of my race, and he wanted to convince his tribe that this was the best way forward. He rather enjoyed liquor and knew the white men gave it out freely in exchange for work. Seeing his hesitation and hoping to save him from any contact with the white traffickers, I told him:

"The words I have spoken to you sprang from my heart, but if you don't want to listen, then simply ignore them and stay with your tribe. However, let me tell you here and now that the men of my race have nothing good to offer you, only a great many ills. As for myself, regardless of your decision, I will go to the Metasboc until the rainy season, when they will have gone away from here again."

"If you go," he answered, "the tribe goes with you. They do not want to be apart from you, for you free us from many evils and they believe you are a kindly god, even if your appearance is that of a white man. And perhaps you are one more Balam of the four winds, and the fifth wind of your race's Cross. Therefore, should you decide to go, we will move our encampment to a place near your home."

Yellow Bird's words caused a strange emotion to stir within me. I, an outcast among my own race, which considered me just a repulsive, better-off-dead drunk, was, in the estimate of these clear-hearted men of the Lacantún, a latter-day Balam, a prophet—practically a god. And that is just what I would be for them, a benevolent spirit who would shower them with blessings. I would teach them the arts, and educate them in settled life, and together we would found a clean, hygienic village where the children could thrive. I would be a latter-day Kukulkan, come to reinvigorate the roots of the Maya, and I would return them to their ancient splendor.

The following day we dismantled the houses and set out on the path to the Metasboc. The women carried the kitchenware and gourds full of food and the packs of corn and yucca; the men carried the weapons and hacked our way forward through the jungle; Yellow Bird toted everything that belonged to the cult of the gods, the censers, and copal; and I brought my notebooks, my rifle, and my desire for a new, expansive life.

IV

A four-day walk brought us to the place Yellow Bird had chosen along the muddy banks of the Metasboc to pitch his tribe's caribal. The site was on a little hill beside a swamp, where the tribe had once lived, many years before: though to an untrained eye it would have looked like any old patch of jungle, you could still see traces of the land they had cleared back then for cultivation. The Lacandon made their encampment at the very top of the hill, while I built my hut down by the lake, where there were sure to be plenty of mosquitoes: for my only concerns in life by that point were the well-being of my friends the Lacandon and my study of the language and customs of these insects. My friends insisted that I set up my brush hut beside their encampment, but I didn't want to and I told them I had to live far away in a solitary place if I was to uphold my contact with the Balams of the winds, but that they should feel free to come visit my home whenever they wanted.

Once I had settled in, I revised my notes and dove back into my studies, worried that the mosquito language here would not be the same as the one spoken along the Lacantún; but on the first night I heard with immense joy that it was the same, after all, and I could repeat my experiments, already familiar with every buzz.

For six months I devoted myself to these studies, interrupted only momentarily every now and then by Yellow Bird or some other tribe member who had come to tell me what they had learned—I never did discover how—about the lumberjacks approaching our old home on the Lacantún. I think those were the happiest days of my life, the days when I lived with the greatest sense of peace, my soul free of any desires beyond doing good, being constructive, and getting up in the morning. At that time my only ambition was to do right by my friends the Lacandon. And I dreamt of bringing three or four disparate tribes together into one great caribal, right there on the fertile banks of the Metasboc, and teaching them how to sow seeds in the earth diligently, how to raise the livestock I would obtain for them. My head was full of well-meaning projects, and I kept up my study of the mosquitoes' language solely out of scientific ambition. I thought of leaving the jungle one day with a stupendous book on mosquitoes, publishing it, and bringing my friends all the things they needed most with the money my book earned. I can guarantee with absolute certainty—the selfsame certainty with which I have recounted my deliriums and illnesses—that my soul was overflowing with goodwill in those days, that I had almost come so far as to cease hating the men of my race, simply fearing them for the negative effects they were capable of having on my friends. I had a vague recollection of my readings on the Jesuit and Franciscan missions of Uruguay and California, and I dreamt of creating something along those lines. I had already run the most difficult part of my course, that is, gaining the confidence of the tribes. The rest would be a cinch.

To help my friends, I began to take care of their emaciated and sickly children. In my hut I gave them extra food and told off-the-cuff stories to entertain them, trying to awaken their slumbering imaginations, although I never mentioned the world beyond the jungle so as not to plant in them the desire to leave and live among the white man. At other times, on days of suffocating heat, we went swimming in the lake and I made them little paper boats to play with. This fun little activity caught on with the adults too, and soon they were all asking me for paper boats to float out on

23

the lake or down some stream. I told them all that the evil spirits sailed away in those boats and I believe they already considered this pastime a ritual.

Yes, those were the happiest days of my life. I see it clearly now, and I weep for having ruined it all, for how my crazed ambition for power overcame the kindness that was only just beginning to dwell in my heart, that new, marvelous, and selfless love the Lacandon had placed in my soul. And now, with death closing in on me as I write this, the book I had wanted to write for the benefit of my friends, I realize that I am still filled with hatred and motivated only by the fear of total annihilation, and I see that those days of poverty, of nothingness, were the only happy ones of my life. But it's too late now. I can't turn back, and regrets are good for nothing.

As for my studies, I had successfully decrypted a handful of Mosquil phrases and was honing my capacity to differentiate between the subtlest shifts in tone and semitone. My nights were fascinating: I spent them listening to the chatter of thousands of mosquitoes, hearing the orders given by the ones who appeared to be their leaders and guarding myself against the rest, insofar as my blood was concerned, the best I could.

I spent eight months composing my *Dictionary of the Mosquil Language*, which I have left in a notebook alongside this one, so all future humans will be able to interpret the language of the mosquitoes with ease and draw up a truce between our species. I hereby deliver to humanity this dictionary (which I once considered destroying to prevent it from falling into the hands of any man at all) as proof that I have forgiven you for all the awful things you did to me, on the one condition that you never forget me. If you are able to draw up a truce with the mosquitoes, which should be simple, a whole new world of cooperation with these so-called inferior beings will be established for our future generations—a world free of a great many diseases and full of wonder.

It is a world I myself have known and that I grant to you, and you will have me to thank for it.

As soon as I understood everything the mosquitoes said, it occurred to me that I might possibly imitate their sounds and, by way of this, speak their language and converse with them. This wasn't as easy as it sounds. The task of speaking in music, in the four vocal ranges, and distinguishing clearly between the semitones, represented great obstacles for me, with my middling knowledge of musical theory. I spent days on end rehearsing even the most rudimentary phrases over and over, but my sounds in no way resembled the ones the mosquitoes made and I was sure that they wouldn't be able to understand me. I decided then that I would have to recreate the sounds with an instrument of some kind, and I went looking through Nocturnal Raccoon's caribal, about four leagues from our own, for Florentino Kimbol, who was renowned as a skilled craftsman of clay flutes and reed whistles. When he saw me, he stood up and asked:

"Is your heart well?"

"Utz," I answered in Maya. "Very much so."

And we sat beside each other in silence. Nocturnal Raccoon's tribe knew me well, each of its members saw me as a friend of their people and held me in high regard. After a while he said to me:

"The white men are making progress and will soon reach the Lacantún. They have come in search of wood, and it grows abundantly here. Look at the trunk of this tree we're sitting on."

"This is mahogany," I said.

"Utz," he replied. "And there is much of it in this jungle. There are big trees, and others that produce rubber."

Having said this, he took out a great cigar of black tobacco and offered it to me. I accepted it and lit it with a coal from the stove, which his wife Petronila brought over to us, and I resumed my silence.

"Did you come through the jungle just now?" he asked.

"Yes," I answered. "I came to see you because my heart desires to speak certain words to you."

"If I had liquor I would offer you a cup," he told me. "But we have distanced ourselves from the men of your race, and they are the ones who bring the alcohol."

"I don't want any alcohol," I told him, "because I know the men of my race hide evil spirits in it to do harm to your people. That's why I persuaded Yellow Bird to move his caribal to the Metasboc, so he wouldn't have to negotiate with the white men."

"My father, Nocturnal Raccoon, also wanted to follow Yellow Bird because he appreciates you and his heart needs you," said Florentino, with a tinge of sadness, "and now I don't have any liquor to offer you."

"Don't be so hard on yourself," I told him. "I don't drink anymore, because I know it's bad." Deep in my soul I felt something pleasant. It wasn't only Yellow Bird who appreciated me: Nocturnal Raccoon and his tribe had also followed in my footsteps. Soon the union could be struck between these two tribes, and my friends' new civilization could begin.

While I thought about these things, Florentino smoked on in silence, spitting from time to time. At last, he spoke:

"You are wise," he told me, "and we liken you to the owl who sees all and never closes his eyes. But there is a sadness in your heart, for you hate the men of your race and keep us far away from them."

"If I try to keep you away from them it is only because I know them and the evil they bring. But I didn't come here to speak of those things, Florentino. I came because I want to make use of your expertise and those hands of yours to carve me a flute."

With his customary discretion, Florentino didn't ask what I wanted it for. Maybe he imagined that I was going to try to summon my gods with it. He simply listened closely to my descriptions and set to work on a thin reed.

After several attempts, he had carved a flute capable of producing every sound I needed, with a tone quite similar to the mosquitoes' buzzing, and once night had fallen I snuck back with it to Yellow Bird's caribal and into my hut.

That very night I tested out my flute and buzzed the word: "Come!"

A mosquito that had been flying around my head froze momentarily and flew away, crying to his fellows that he had heard a voice calling to him. This initial experiment fired up my enthusiasm, for his reaction showed me the mosquitoes could understand what I was saying, or buzzing, and so I kept on practicing with even greater resolve. But the further I penetrated the different aspects of the language, the harder it seemed to produce all the required tones and semitones with the necessary precision.

In a third notebook (which I have left alongside this one and the one with my dictionary), I have written out all the essential points of Mosquil usage, that is, all the most important grammatical rules. It must be noted that this language has no exceptions to its rules, which makes it the most civilized language I have ever encountered.

After many rehearsals, believing that practice makes perfect, I felt I had worked up sufficient knowledge and ability to strike up a conversation with the mosquitoes, and I started it one night, with one who was flying around my head and singing a tune that seemed to be popular among them.

"Come!" I said to him in the deep tone of command; then in the high-pitched imperative tone: "Don't go, I only want to talk to you."

The mosquito was startled and let out three or four exclamations in the soprano range, looking around to find the mosquito who was addressing him.

"Listen to me," I said again in the deep tone of command. "I'm the one talking to you, the man you have been tormenting."

And the mosquito landed momentarily on a rope of my hammock.

"From what I ascertain, you have learned our language," he said to me. "And I must respect and obey you, per orders of the High Council that governs us and whose name I mustn't pronounce. Order me as you will, and I shall obey."

I was a little confused, not knowing what order to give, nor how to begin our conversation. Moreover, to be perfectly honest, my excitement was almost preventing me from being able to buzz with my flute at all.

"If you don't want anything from me, why did you call me?" the mosquito asked me, disturbed by my indecision.

"I have no orders to give you," I replied. "I only called you over so we could talk."

The mosquito seemed to hesitate for a moment until he finally buzzed:

"Pardon my hesitation, but I do not believe I am the right one of us for you to speak to, because I am of a lower caste: a mere scout. I do not know what to do in this situation, and I must notify my superior immediately, who will notify his superior, and so on until the message reaches the High Council of this zone. But I am afraid to do so, because I have never heard of any other being in creation capable of speech, and I worry that all of this is but a dream."

"This is no dream. I have studied your language for years, and now—"

"So you were the one who spoke recently to a comrade, who said he had heard voices and was executed for it."

"Yes, I spoke to him: I said, 'Come!' and he flew away screaming, terrified. I am sorry to learn of his death . . ."

"Death doesn't matter," he answered me. "What matters is the success of our mission, moving the project forward, and I believe the fact that you have learned our language—that, for the first time, we can make ourselves understood to another being of creation—is of great importance. So I will call my superior, and I ask you to speak to him, to make sure this doesn't cost me my life."

"Summon him," I told him, "and do not be afraid."

And so he did, buzzing loudly, and shortly after his superior presented himself, a perfect anopheles who appeared indignant when he learned why he had been called. So I spoke to him myself:

"Do not punish your subordinate," I told him. "He has done nothing but speak the truth, and I asked him to call you so you could decide what is to be done. I have learned your language: I have studied it for years, and I want to speak with you and be your friend, rather than your enemy."

"You have never been our enemy," answered the superior insect. "We the mosquitoes, the masters of all things, have no enemies. You have served us as a blood source to feed the High Council, whose name I mustn't pronounce, for it is too lofty for me to utter—"

"But I have killed so many of you."

"The death of a few bodies doesn't matter. Your blood was essential to us, and we took it. If you had killed a hundred times more, we still would have taken it."

"How delightful," I answered him with much finesse, but very little truth. "I want to be your friend."

"We have neither friends nor enemies, but since you have learned our language and we can talk to you, perhaps you can be of some use to us." Then, turning toward the mosquito who had spoken first, he said, "You have done well to have called me. I will recommend you to be named Guard of the Great Treasury."

"How delightful," I intervened. "I would not have liked for this poor mosquito to suffer an unjust punishment, like the one before."

"You place too much importance on death, which means nothing to us. But it would be good for the two of you to continue your conversation. I will gather all of my superiors, so they may decide how best to bring this matter before the High Council and see what is to be done."

And having said this, he buzzed aloud and there appeared those large mosquitoes I had seen before. Several hundred of them appeared, and after hearing his words, filled the air with such a din of buzzing that I felt I had to address them to calm them down. So, taking out my flute, I said to them:

"My good sirs, this captain is speaking the truth. I have learned this language in order to be able to speak with you. I don't see it as cause for calamity."

"You don't understand what you're saying," one of the large mosquitoes told me. "This is the single most important event that has ever taken place in our history, which spans hundreds of thousands of years. Your arrival may in fact be providential, but I mustn't speak of such things without first immediately notifying this zone's High Council so that it, in turn, may notify all the High Councils in the world and the Supreme Council may be convened, something that has not happened for five hundred eighty-six thousand years, seven months, and fourteen days. That is what I must do ..."

And having said this, he flew off, trailed by all the other mosquitoes, and left my hut empty, so empty that the murmur of the jungle reached through the gaps in the palm leaves, as if trying to touch me. In the meantime, I waited.

V

The Lacandon children arrived at dawn, hoping to go for a swim with me and to cast little paper boats off in the river's current. I went with them and the cool, murky waters cleared my mind, and I was able to meditate in peace on what had taken place the night before. There was no doubt that I had achieved something no other man had ever achieved before, something so extraordinary that it would bring me fame throughout all future generations, and my name would never be forgotten. Finally I could return to the world and spit my disdain in everyone's face. I, the better-off-dead drunk, had achieved more than all the scientists, power mongers, wise men, biologists, and scholars of inferior species combined. Maybe I would found an institute—which, naturally, would bear my name—devoted to the study of all animal languages.

But every aspect of the night before still seemed like a dream to me. I had to be completely sure, to speak with the mosquitoes in the light of day, to learn about their customs, their lives, their history, to try and forge an alliance so they might finally stop plaguing mankind, and bring this pact before the human race as the invaluable gift it was. But would people thank me for what I was doing on their behalf? Mankind has always despised truly great men; it has done so a thousand times before, and will continue doing so—but not with me. My discovery would give me such power that everyone would be forced to respect me and I would know how to take control and make them treat me accordingly. Perhaps I could keep a number of mosquito squadrons to act as my security detail and put my achievements on display. The study of a whole new branch of science would be undertaken: the studies of animal language. I would give it a Greek name, though at the time I couldn't think of a good one, maybe something like zoophonology.

Suddenly, I realized that in all my dreams of such lofty subjects, I had forgotten all about the children shouting at me to make them more little boats. Getting up from the sand, where I had been lounging, I walked over to the water to fold more, and was met with cries of youthful jubilation. It was then that I decided never to abandon my Lacandon friends, but to help turn them into a civilized people, all while conserving their elemental character, their candor, their goodness: I would use the money I made from my discovery to make sure of it.

While the children were off chasing the little boats, I lay back down upon the sand, in the shade of a nearby bay cedar. All of a sudden I heard a mosquito buzzing and almost swatted it out of instinct, but without any conscious effort I began to understand what it was saying to me.

"Certain members of the High Council, the name of which we mustn't utter, have sent me to greet you and inform you they would like to speak with you by proxy of one of their ambassadors."

"And why don't they speak to me directly?" I asked, using my flute.

"You mustn't understand what you've just said. The High Council, whose name we are not allowed to pronounce and which only a select few of us know, never speaks with anyone except the head of the transmitters, or ambassadors. He, in turn, elects one of his subordinates to decide who is to carry the High Council's pronouncements, and certain other subordinates, named record-keepers, then learn these pronouncements and repeat them forever so they may never be forgotten."

"Even in a case as important as this?" I asked, trying to understand the mosquitoes' organization more fully.

"This is the most important case in our entire history, which spans more than five hundred thousand years; even so, the High Council will not speak to you directly. The recordkeepers have already repeated the words the council has deemed necessary for this case, and all heard those words that demonstrated that major events will be taking place. I believe the ambassador, or transmitter, wants to make these pronouncements known to you."

"Send him posthaste," I said.

The mosquito took flight, vanishing into the trees, and within a few seconds several large mosquitoes arrived buzzing loudly, trailed by a male anopheles. He landed on a little stick beside my head, and I readied my flute.

"The High Council," he said, "whose name I mustn't pronounce, has sent me here to wish you prosperity among your fellow men and such glory that you will not be forgotten when you die and your name will be repeated by future generations until the end of all endings."

"Thank you," I answered. "Please express my gratitude to the High Council for its warm wishes. I do not know what I could possibly wish it in return, or how to properly express my greetings, but before you tell me the message they have entrusted you with, I would like to say a few words. I believe this is the first time a human has spoken with you and that mutual comprehension has been achieved between the mosquitoes and mankind. I want peace between our races to spring from this comprehension; for you to stop plaguing man, and for humans to stop killing mosquitoes with the many tools they have invented for this purpose."

As soon as I finished speaking, several of the large mosquitoes, who had arrived before the transmitter, began to buzz, repeating what I had said, and once they had finished they flew off again into the shadows of the jungle. Then the transmitter spoke again:

"The High Council, whose name I mustn't pronounce, has informed me that from this day forth you will be assigned designated recordkeepers, so none of your words may ever be lost. This is the first time that such an honor has been granted, and you should feel proud. The recordkeepers accompanying me will now convey to you the words the High Council has chosen from among all those in existence." After saying this, he fell silent and one of the recordkeepers proclaimed:

"Hear the word of the High Council, the word entrusted to me! Rational animals being few in the universe, the kingdom of mosquitoes must form an alliance with another in order to achieve its goals. So said the High Council, four hundred thirty-two thousand six hundred fifty-nine years, three months, and two days ago."

Just as he finished, another one said:

"Hear the word of the High Council, the word entrusted to me! Among all other extant races in the world, we believe the human race to be the most reasonable, and we must seek an alliance with it once it has achieved sufficient organization. So said the High Council, four thousand seven hundred twenty-two years, five months, and nineteen days ago."

And another one said, just as that mosquito finished:

"Hear the word of the High Council, the word entrusted to me! Humans have progressed and learned a great deal. They must be monitored closely, since they may prove useful to us. So said the High Council, three hundred twenty-four years, nine months, and one day ago."

Since no other mosquito made to speak, I pressed my flute to my lips and said:

"It brings me immense pleasure to learn that the High Council has desired to form an alliance with humanity for so many innumerable years. I believe I can be the intermediary for such an alliance and, if you grant me sufficient power, I can broker a complete agreement."

"The High Council," answered the transmitter, "has already considered every possibility and is aware of everything it needs to know at this time. The High Council does nothing but think and there is no possible situation for which it does not already have a plan. But before dealing with you and your species, it would like you to study our way of life and government, to immerse yourself in its perfection so that you may then bring our message before mankind."

"Excellent," I answered him. "Nothing would bring me more pleasure than to understand your social organization."

"The recordkeepers will bring you the High Council's word and I am sure it will please you. Here, you have these comrades, who have been specially appointed to tell you everything you need to know. May your name remain in the annals of the coming generations."

And having finished, he disappeared with his mob of recordkeepers, buzzing gloriously to document what I had said. Only twenty large mosquitoes stayed behind; and one of them, who seemed to be their leader, said to me:

"My name is easy to remember, it is Good Sun. The council has appointed me to instruct you, along with these twenty comrades under my command. We belong to the Logic branch and our function consists in knowing everything, in joining together the scattered pieces of new information brought back by the scouts with all the knowledge preserved by the recordkeepers, and deducing from this all the conclusions the council must be made aware of."

"From what I can tell," I said, "you have many different categories, each with a designated occupation."

"Correct," he answered. "We have many diverse branches, which are united in a single body: the Great Center, which is governed by the council. Every mosquito has his own occupation, and he inherits its knowledge and expands it: he lives and dies in it. Starting from the bottom up, there is the branch of scouts, whose mission is to locate the sites where there is food for the council and to lead the suppliers there—suppliers being females exempt from rearing larvae, and who also form part of the lowest rank. Scouts and suppliers can both be promoted to posts in the security force that guards the treasury, of which we will speak in due time. Above them are the captains, who are in charge of inspecting the work performed by their inferiors, rounding up or putting down the wounded, according to whether or not they are carrying blood, and to seek out secure locations for the treasury. Another branch is in charge of the accounts. These mosquitoes have to keep track of the quantity of members in each corpus, how many casualties have been suffered, and how many more will be necessary at any given time. For example, when you used to kill our scouts and suppliers, the captains notified their accountants immediately, so they would be able to replace these subjects and ensure that the units were always complete and able to control and monitor this entire jungle entrusted to our corpus."

"So there are other corpora beyond your own?" I asked.

"Yes, there are three hundred thousand distinct corpora in the world, each of which takes its orders from a legislative body even higher than the High Council of which you have heard tell. This Supreme Council is composed of one member from every High Council, each of which has one hundred ten elected members, who in turn elect eleven to rule, and whose decisions are not subject to appeal. But to return to the lower branches, there are others whose sole responsibility it is to gather the blood carried by the suppliers and deliver it to the High Council, which uses this blood as its exclusive food. The members of the feeder branch seize the suppliers, kill them, suck their blood, and transfer it to the Unnameable Members."

"It seems cruel to me to kill the suppliers like that," I interrupted.

"I don't see why. The name of the one they kill is given to another, so she never dies. Besides, her corpse remains in the great treasury for the duration of its usefulness. Another division is the army of offensive attack. When any other being interferes with us, we attack it with this army, which has many different weapons. Some inject a poison that causes swelling and itchiness, while some transmit malaria, yellow fever, or river blindness, depending on the case at hand. Others carry diseases unknown to humans as of yet. Thanks to this division, we have been able to hold enormous swaths of jungle, where we keep our treasury and High Council."

"In many places," I intervened, "people have been able to drive those armies back, rendering them harmless."

"It is true that we have suffered defeats, but the great battle has yet to be waged, and from it we shall emerge victorious. But let us speak of that later. For now, meditate upon what I have told you and keep it in your memory."

And having said this, he vanished. The Lacandon children were heading home along the beach, sad about how all their little boats had sunk. We folded some more, which suffered the same fate, and I went off to rest in my hut.

VI

It was in that way, by talking with the transmitters and record-keepers, that I gradually learned about the mosquitoes' complex world. On top of their immense system of departments, there are also what they call the "Great Treasury" and the "Arsenal." The Great Treasuries are hidden away in caves and, as far as I understand, every mosquito corpus scattered across the world organizes itself in the same way. These treasuries preserve an incalculable number of larvae in ideal conditions to be converted into mosquitoes whenever more are called for. The Great Treasury of the Metasboc Corpus, the corpus I was in contact with, had more than a hundred billion larvae of all species ready to be hatched whenever necessary. In addition to that, the suppliers laid about a million more eggs every day. The treasury was under the care of a special branch with its own corpus of accountants that kept a constant count of the number of larvae in existence. I was never allowed to see it myself, nor did they tell me where the caves were located, but it is my understanding that they can be found by the banks of the Metasboc, tucked away behind certain huge boulders, near the High Council's residence.

The arsenals are kept elsewhere, generally on a lake where the mosquitoes of the military branch incubate and protect the germs they use as weapons. They go there to stock up on these germs and spread them wherever they are instructed to. There is a special subdivision whose task it is to raise and feed those germs, and a portion of the blood the suppliers suck is set aside for these purposes. As far as I understand, there is enough malaria and yellow fever in the Metasboc Arsenal alone to kill more than two hundred million humans, and it is capable of producing enough germs per day to kill a million more. They breed other germs, such as *Onchocerca volvulus*, in trees they reserve expressly for that purpose, principally coffee trees, but they use them very little in comparison to malaria, which seems to be their weapon of choice.

To breed this microbe they use what they refer to as "live arsenals"—simply the bloodstream of a living human or animal. A mosquito injects its germs and leaves them there to reproduce, marking the human or animal with signs recognizable only by other mosquitoes. If the human goes anywhere else, the mosquitoes of that region will recognize him as a live arsenal and know that his blood will make for a tremendous food source for the High Council.

On several occasions throughout history, humans have succeeded in destroying the arsenal or treasury of some mosquito corpus or other—as happened with the three Panamanian corpora, which the High Council of Metasboc often cites as an example. These corpora have had to request aid in order to rebuild these establishments, which are being reconstructed to this day in more remote locations.

As for the internal structure of the individual corpora, I ascertained that they each function as a single unit, and that the individual mosquitoes that compose the *corpus*—I have chosen the Latin word for *body* to translate this governmental concept, of course, for exactly this double meaning—resemble the human body's cells, each with its own function. The High Council is this body's brain, the transmitters its nerves, the recordkeepers its memory. The Great Treasury is the reproductive system, the suppliers the cells that gather food from the human's gut, and the army is what medicine, I believe, calls antitoxins, since its particular mission is to defend the corpus, the High Council in particular. As such, the death of one mosquito is only as important to an entire corpus as the death of one cell is to an entire human. In truth, every individual unit of mosquitoes is a being unto itself, just like a human being, but these units enjoy the distinct advantage that each of their cells has a life of its own and isn't bound to the space occupied by a single body, but is instead able to venture off wherever it pleases. In this, they have a leg up, because when they go off in search of food they don't have to drag the entire body along: they dispatch only the necessary cells, and this principle applies to every other activity in their lives. And so, with a single body, they are able to perform all necessary tasks at once.

There are some three hundred thousand units like this on earth, each spanning a radius of greater or lesser magnitude, depending on its strength. There are some, according to Good Sun, that cover hundreds of square miles of jungle, and others—the ones in cold countries—that thrive only in the summer and don't maintain arsenals; these cover much smaller areas, some only the surface of a single pond.

A union exists between all these corpora, which are governed by one all-powerful council, as I have already explained—a supreme council that has not been convened in the past five hundred thousand years, ever since peace was achieved between all mosquitoes around the world. In order to understand this, however, a bit of history will be necessary.

There was once a time when each mosquito corpus was composed of a single unit, its cells interconnected like those of the human body. These monsters lived in a state of everlasting war and expended all their creative energy on seeking out weapons to attack and defend themselves. One of these corpora discovered that noxious germs could be used as weapons, and employed this tactic to wreak death and destruction upon the other corpora, eventually bringing them under its control and governing them tyrannically for thousands of years. At last, one of the oppressed

corpora thought to do away with much of its body's bulk, scatter-
ing its cells and granting them lives of their own, which ensured
that only one mosquito at a time would get sick and die. Pursuing
these discoveries further, they managed to structure their corpora as they do today, as immortal bodies that can't reproduce
to create novel bodies, so their number has always been limited
to their original amount. Once they had dispersed their cells and
the mosquitoes flew freely, they quickly overthrew the tyrant but
continued warring amongst themselves, until about five hundred
thousand years ago, when they realized the absurdity of such endless infighting, and decided it would be best to divvy up the globe.
So the Supreme Council was convened to carry out this division:
it drew up a statute, declaring that every mosquito corpus, regardless of its size, would have the right to some part of the earth,
and that location assignments would be decided at random. The
largest corpora immediately revolted, claiming that it would only
be fair for them to choose their location first, and since they based
their proposal on force, the council had no choice but to approve
it. So, the major corpora took the places they saw fit—hot places
in particular, where they could find more food and did not have
to suffer the cold. The minor corpora settled down wherever they
could, some of them going very far north, all the way to Alaska, in
search of lakes where they could live in peace.

From that day forth, the Supreme Council had never been
convened again, and each corpus assumed its designated place
with a free internal government. All the High Councils continued
to communicate with one another through a global network of
emissaries, who let themselves be carried along, I suppose, by the
jet streams, of which they are experts.

By now, the majority of the corpora have outgrown their
sites and been obligated, by the lack of space and food for such
population growth, to reduce their larva reserves, though they
still conserve a large portion of their treasuries. Humans have

contributed in part to this scarcity of food and space by deforesting vast expanses of jungle, killing off nearly all the wildlife, and developing many areas. There are corpora who have lost nearly all their territory and live wretchedly, with a monumental treasury and a stunted corpus.

When a corpus decides to increase in size, its accountants calculate the requisite number of individuals from each species, pay a visit to the treasury, extract the necessary larvae, and raise them. When, on the contrary, they decide to decrease in size, they let the excess cells die and allocate all larvae laid by the females to the treasury. The corpora increase and decrease in size annually according to the seasons in the cold climates, and according to food in the warm climates. In the Metasboc Corpus, which is without a doubt among the most important in the world, the accountants go to the treasury three weeks before fruit season begins and extract several million female larvae. When they are born, these females have no trouble finding food and lay a great quantity of eggs, which go to the treasury. When these suppliers die, they are not replaced.

Certain posts still exist—those of the three thousand members of the High Council—reserved entirely for thinking. Since they have spent five hundred thousand years in thought, they have already imagined an answer to any situation that may possibly present itself, no matter how strange, and all those answers reside in the memory of the recordkeepers—another post that never terminates. And as the High Council has already thought of every response to every situation and no novel situation can present itself to them, I believe they may by now have given in to sloth in their caves and do hardly more than approve the accountants' tallies.

I learned all that history from Good Sun and his recordkeepers, who merely repeated the words the council had entrusted them with. I struck up a great friendship with the first Good Sun and all the Good Suns who took his place successively as each one died—for a mosquito lives only briefly and the one who replaces him assumes his name and every trait; and while he taught me of the lives and customs of mosquitoes, I taught him of humans, describing the myriad things people have invented to protect themselves. I knew my friend was an important member of the corpus, because he was the head or chief of the logicians.

During that whole time I spent immersed in study, my friends the Lacandon never dared interrupt me: whenever they saw me alone, always with my lips pressed to my flute, they believed I was in communion with the good spirits. Sometimes the children came to swim with me, but although we shared an old camaraderie, they seemed hesitant to ask me to make them little paper boats, so I taught them how to fold their own, and I gave them sheets of paper from my notebooks. Once a day, in the morning, Black Ant brought me my pozol of cornmeal in water, tidied up my hut, and left without a word—but I could see in her eyes the nagging question: Why don't you kill mosquitoes for your medicine anymore?

One day I said to her:

"Black Ant, my sister, you have come to my house for many days in a row now, and I can tell you haven't asked me what you want to know."

"It's true," she told me. "You know all, Wise Owl. Answer my question, then."

"You want to know why I no longer kill mosquitoes at night, like I used to. And I'll tell you. The mosquitoes are no longer my enemy. They have become my friends, and I want them to be your friends, just as they are mine. I will have a word with them, and you will be able to sleep wherever you like without being bothered; and the fevers and chills will go away, too, and you won't have to fill your huts with smoke anymore, or buy the white men's candles to fight off the mosquitoes."

Somewhat perplexed, Black Ant looked at me and left without a word. Immediately I took out my flute and called to Good Sun.

"I have never asked the High Council for a favor," I told him. "Now I want them to grant me one."

"It is not the custom of the High Council, whose name I mustn't pronounce, to grant any favors," he answered me. "We have never heard of anyone making such a request, but if they have already thought of a favorable answer to what you are going to ask, it will be granted."

"What I will ask is simple, and I believe that the council, if it hasn't already thought of an answer to this situation, can easily think one up—"

"You mustn't understand what you're saying," Good Sun interrupted me. "The High Council no longer thinks of new answers, especially in cases of great urgency."

"So what good is it?"

"It is the High Council," he told me. "Ask what you will, and you will receive its answer."

"What I want is simple. I would only like for you to stop torturing that small group of people who live beside me and who are my friends. I want you to refrain from biting them, so they can stay healthy, and to stop bothering them with your buzzing."

"I will bring your question before the council, but know that even if your friends are granted freedom from the bondage of the blood tribute they owe us—we do tolerate their presence in our territory, after all—they may not be granted the same protection that you have been granted."

It was then I realized that the High Council had gone to the effort of stationing various mosquito squadrons to protect me, scaring away all the animals that could hurt me.

Shortly after, Good Sun returned with a recordkeeper, who buzzed:

"Hear the High Council's word, the word entrusted to me! If

any foreign being of creation should learn our language and be able to communicate with us, we shall protect him, provided this being is of some use to us, and we shall protect the individuals of his choosing, provided they are of a limited number. So said the High Council, four hundred and twenty-two years, nine months, and two days ago."

"Now you have heard," said Good Sun. "Your friends will no longer be made to pay the blood tribute they owe us, and they will not be bothered."

I thanked him to the best of my ability, though I was a little disturbed by all this about blood tributes and how they would protect me only as long as I was of use to them. "Of what use?" I thought. "To forge an alliance with the humans?"

That night, not a single mosquito bothered my friends the Lacandon in their caribal. The next day Black Ant didn't dare enter my hut and left my food at the door, bowing deeply as she withdrew. Shortly after, Yellow Bird arrived and set down the jugs that were his gods upon the table; he was wearing his red head-band, a sign that he was a high priest. After murmuring several prayers, he blessed me with copal and, kneeling before me, said:

"Wise Owl, who sees and knows all, from Black Ant we have learned of your powers, your greatness, your goodness, how you have succeeded in bringing under your dominion the evil spirts who once tormented us in the night. This is why I believe you are Kukulkan, the white, the bearded, who has returned to his people, and I bring you our gods so they may keep you company. All I can possibly do is to ask you to stay forever in my caribal, and to teach me the art of making my people happy."

I was stunned to have been deified by his speech, and before I could reply Yellow Bird had already crept out of my hut, never once turning his back on me, leaving behind his gods and a clump of smoking copal.

VII

I spent two months, give or take, in talks with my friend Good Sun, learning about the mosquito kingdom's political organization and perfecting my grasp of their language. I didn't take any notes, because I didn't have the time and because I was too astonished and excited by everything I was hearing to write it down, but I remember it all just as well as if I learned it yesterday.

Good Sun also kept me abreast of the High Council members and their daily activities; and although I hinted on several occasions that I would have liked to speak to them directly, my petition was never taken into account or so much as acknowledged by Good Sun, and I decided not to push the point.

The High Council had appealed to the Supreme Council and dispatched emissaries to every mosquito kingdom or corpus scattered around the globe to tell them of the news. According to what Good Sun told me, the Supreme Council had agreed to convene in order to consider my affair, although he never did explain exactly what this "affair" entailed.

I supposed it was a matter of striking a truce with mankind, but I had heard things I wasn't quite thrilled to hear, like all this about the Lacandon having to pay a blood tribute. Moreover, the sense of superiority with which they always spoke gave me the impression that they considered humans inferior beings, however much I insinuated that mosquitoes were, in fact, the inferior creature.

For the time being, I spoke only with Good Sun and listened to the recordkeepers to make sure my words had been understood.

Twice or three times, while I was walking through the jungle, I noticed mosquito squadrons behind me and ahead of me, scaring away all the animals that could hurt me—snakes in particular and other crawling things. One night a jaguar roared near my door and a number of squadrons appeared and attacked it so badly the poor thing had to run for its life.

One morning I was talking to Good Sun with my flute, when Nocturnal Raccoon and Florentino appeared in my doorway. They stopped at the threshold and fell to their knees as they watched me play. I got up to encourage them to stand, but couldn't convince them to rise until they had kissed my hands and placed an offering of meat, honey, and fruit at my feet.

"Forgive us, O Wise Owl, Good Balam!" said Nocturnal Raccoon, "for having arrived at your door without shouting from afar as is our custom, but since we now know you are the all-knowing Kukulkan, we didn't believe it necessary to announce our presence. We beg you to accept our humble offerings."

He fell back down to his knees as he said this. I stepped forward and tried to pick him up by the arm, setting my flute down on the table next to the jars that were Yellow Bird's gods, and which I had not been able to get him to come take back; at which point Florentino fell to his knees again in adoration of the flute he had crafted with his own hands.

After another round of divine and human courtesies, I was able to coax them back to their feet. Standing before me, Nocturnal Raccoon spoke:

"We have come to ask something of you, O White Kukulkan!"

Before he could get back on his knees, I said:

"Ask what you wish and, if I am able, I will make it so. For you and your people have been my friends and are near to my heart."

"We want you to allow us to set up our village beside your hut, wherever you say, so we, along with Yellow Bird and his village, can care for you and provide you with food."

Florentino nodded his head to his father's every word with such enthusiasm that he almost snapped his neck. I remained deep in thought for a moment, imagining what Yellow Bird would think if this tribe and I became neighbors; at last, I told them:

"I would like you to build your caribal beside Yellow Bird's, and for your tribes to join together as one. If you do, you will enjoy my protection, as Yellow Bird's village already does, and I will liberate you from the evil spirits. And so, I want ..."

"You do not want, O Kukulkan! You command," Florentino interjected.

"Well, then," I said. "I command you to build your village at the foot of the hill beside Yellow Bird, and to live united as family. Go on, Florentino, my brother, and call for Yellow Bird, because I want to tell him what I have decided, too ..."

Florentino ran off and returned in no time with my friend the chief, who had been nearby, spying, I believe, on Nocturnal Raccoon and Florentino's doings in my hut. Once I explained what the visitors had in mind, his face lost its cheer and he fell silent for a while.

"What says your heart? Is my proposal good?"

"Utz," he answered me. "Everything you say is good, for you are Kukulkan, the white, the bearded, the good."

"All I want," I told him, "is for the two tribes to join together as one and for all to treat each other as family."

There was a moment of silence, during which each chief reflected on what he wanted to say. Finally, Yellow Bird spoke: "Who, O Good Balam! will rule that great tribe?"

"Who do you believe should rule it?" I asked him.

"I should," he answered. "We established ourselves here first. This is our land; we have been friends to you—"

"But I am your elder, Yellow Bird," Nocturnal Raccoon interrupted. "The power falls to me."

"Yes," said Florentino, "it should go to my father. He is the elder, and the more prosperous."

Even before they could strike a union, the thirst for power had already torn them apart. I knew I had to take on a commanding attitude, or all my dreams of uniting and civilizing the Lacandon would fall to pieces, so I stood up and said:

"Yellow Bird will take command of the tribe. That is my command and that is the opinion of the good spirits I speak to with my flute. Nocturnal Raccoon will be second in charge, and when Yellow Bird quits the caribal, Nocturnal Raccoon will become chief."

The three Lacandon fell silent, Yellow Bird smiling, and the other two upset and on the verge of rebelling and walking back to their homes. To avoid this, and remembering that Yellow Bird had no children, I said:

"Once the two chiefs have reunited with their elders, Florentino will become chief. If you accept my proposal, the spirits say they will make you powerful and that you will become the fathers of a great nation. If you do not accept it, they will resume their previous state and you will be haunted by spirits far crueler than before."

There was a long silence, which ended when Nocturnal Raccoon hesitantly said:

"I am the elder and the more prosperous, and the power falls to me. If you do not grant me this, I cannot accept the union of the tribes, because I will become a laughingstock in my village."

"I have nephews who should inherit this position," said Yellow Bird. "It is unjust to steal away the power that is rightfully theirs upon my death and grant it to these men who have only just arrived."

We debated for two hours without coming to an agreement, no matter how I leveraged my authority. But at long last, Yellow Bird agreed that Florentino should inherit his command, along with one of his brothers, or nephews, if the former were to die; Nocturnal Raccoon, however, would have none of it. He felt he was the natural born chief and wouldn't let anyone twist his arm.

At last, in anger, I sent them to their houses, threatening them with a thousand plagues of mosquitoes and evil spirits.

As soon as they left, I told Good Sun about what was happening. He had a good laugh, and discoursed on the flaws of mankind's organization, since the power invested in every individual was equal to that of every other and the only way this power could go uncontested was if the ones wielding it were stronger than their neighbors or so essential that the latter's very existence depended on them. Rather piqued by the scene with the Lacandon and the mosquito's taunting, I answered:

"You only say all that because you know nothing of mankind's organization. Any human can rise to power, climbing every rung of the ladder. We're not like you, who are the slaves of some outdated council that doesn't even think anymore because everything's already been thought for it—you would do yourselves a favor by dissolving it, so you could live free and strong."

Without a word Good Sun flew off chuckling, and I was left alone with my impotent rage, thinking about how I might be able to follow through on my threat to the Lacandon, unconvinced the mosquitoes would grant me another favor.

VIII

Good Sun arrived at night, as usual, to pay me a visit. I took out my flute and began talking to him, unsure how to broach the subject of my friends the Lacandon. I wanted several mosquito squadrons to attack both villages that very night and give the tribes such a sound thrashing that there would be no doubt about whether or not my curse would come true. Good Sun also seemed nervous and distracted: his words were disjointed and his thoughts seemed far away, completely detached from my friends the Lacandon and the classes he was giving me on the mosquitoes' social organization. Suddenly he said to me, cutting off another train of thought:

"You know, human, the Supreme Council is gathering tonight, something that hasn't taken place in five hundred thousand years."

"That should be quite interesting."

"Yes," he answered. "The High Council has arranged everything. To be more specific, it arranged everything approximately three hundred forty years ago, according to what I heard a record-keeper say—"

"As always, the council has already resolved everything," I interrupted. "I think the recordkeepers are really all you need by now. The purpose of the council was to think and now it has already thought of everything; it seems a bit excessive—"

"Let's not speak of that," Good Sun interrupted. "In fact, a situation has arisen for which the High Council has no answer."

"Well, well, well!" I cried. "What are you going to do now?"

"You can help us. Here's the situation: the Supreme Council—the Unnameable—has more than two million members that survive on blood. So, according to the laws of hospitality, we have to provide for them, because they travel alone, without suppliers or security forces. The ancient tradition cited by the High Council says that, in the beginning, the corpora or units convened the Supreme Council at every juncture. In those times every member of the Supreme Council traveled with a great retinue, seeking provisions along the way, until it was decided that the corpus calling for the meeting must provide blood for the Supreme Council, whose members were no longer to travel with suppliers. Ever since that law was put into effect, no other corpus has convened the Supreme Council, perhaps to save themselves the expense and effort."

"A wise law," I remarked. "If mankind gathered less often to address global affairs, things would be going much better."

"Humans have such limited experience," he told me. "Maybe someday you will achieve our level of perfection and come to understand these things. For now, as I understand it, your individual desire for power and possession is so great that you all lie awake at night biting your nails over government posts, and this renders your lives unbearable. But no need to lose hope, you'll learn. I have faith—I must, to keep myself from feeling sad."

"You still haven't told me how I can help you with all that," I said, to distract him from his sound criticism of human government.

"Several days ago, the High Council ordered the accountants to extract one hundred million supplier larvae and one million scout larvae from the treasury and raise them, in order to feed the members of the Supreme Council; it was done, and they are all already hard at work."

"Good forethought on the part of the High Council," I interrupted.

"But they've run into some problems in carrying out their

tasks. Our main source of food was going to be the blood of your friends from the tribes but we have promised you not to touch them. And the blood of the animals and men who live four leagues away will not suffice."

He fell silent for a while, as I thought of how greatly this could benefit my plans, but I wanted to be sure the command to attack the Lacandon came from him, not me. At last, he said:

"The Supreme Council is meeting because of you and it would be good of you to help us through this difficulty. You must allow us to take just a bit of blood from your friends."

This was exactly what I had been waiting for—I could punish the Lacandon and submit them to my authority. So I answered him, after a moment of feigned reflection:

"My primary interest is to help you and be your friend. Besides, it would be good for those men to give a bit of blood. You may tell the High Council I authorize your attack on these Lacandon—"

"It will be an attack the likes of which have never been seen before," Good Sun interrupted me. "Millions of suppliers will descend upon them—"

"All I ask," I interposed, "is that you not infect them with any diseases. The mosquitoes who attack must not spread any harmful bacteria to the tribes."

"They won't," he replied. "And on behalf of the High Council, I thank you for what you have done, and assure you it will not be forgotten. Now I shall go give the necessary orders..."

"Wait a moment," I told him. "I also want to help provide blood to the members of the Supreme Council. I'll kill a deer or some other large animal and give you the blood."

"We thank you," he told me. "But keep in mind the blood must come from a living creature, because it's useless to us once it has died."

Something cruel occurred to me then, an act I still regret.

"I'll wound a deer," I told him, "and bring him here so you can collect his blood as it pours out."

I went out as midnight was approaching and set myself up by a big pond where I knew the deer liked to drink. Shortly after, one strutted past me; I took my rifle and shot it, aiming for its hind legs.

The animal fell, moaning with a human pathos, as deer do, and I sprang upon it. I threw it over my shoulders and carried it to the door of my hut, despite its desperate kicking.

When I passed by Yellow Bird's caribal, I noticed they had lit great, billowing bonfires to ward off the mosquitoes, and that no one was asleep. With a smile on my face, I arrived at my hut and laid the wounded deer down at the door. Good Sun was already waiting for me there and, behind him, a large company of suppliers. A constant stream of blood flowed from the wound, and they descended upon it, blackening it within a minute. As soon as these suppliers had filled their bellies, others arrived. The poor deer kicked and tried to stand up, moaning every now and then. Good Sun told me:

"Tie up its hooves. We'll be able to finish faster that way." Without a word, I did what I was told. The moon was full, casting enough light to see clearly. Suddenly, the blood stopped flowing.

"Is it dead?" Good Sun asked me.

"No," I answered. "But the blood has clotted and isn't flowing anymore."

"Make it flow," he commanded.

I took my knife and reopened the wound. The deer watched me with big sad eyes, as if begging for death, but in its gaze was neither anger nor hatred: there was only sadness, a sadness so profound I couldn't stand to see it anymore and had to lay a rag over its head. Meanwhile, millions of mosquitoes continued arriving to suck its blood; and, as soon as they had their fill, they left. Suddenly, Good Sun said:

"We've taken enough. Keep it alive—we will require more tomorrow night."

"I can't," I told him. "It horrifies me to watch it suffer. I want to put it out of its misery right now."

"That's because you're human and you only suffer from what you can see. Why weren't you horrified when you killed so many suppliers back when you were our enemy?"

"It wasn't the same," I told him.

"You simply couldn't see their suffering faces. But do as you wish. Tomorrow we will need more blood."

Having said this, he left, followed by his company now gorged with blood. I took my knife and killed the deer, skinned it, and hung its meat up to dry, then laid myself to rest.

The sun still hadn't risen when Yellow Bird arrived with his tribe in tow. It was clear they hadn't been able to sleep all night, and their eyes were swollen. The children were crying. They all stopped before my door and fell to their knees. Yellow Bird was the first to speak:

"We have disobeyed you, O Wise Owl! you, who are our friend, who are a good Balam who has come to visit us, who are Kukulkan, the wise, the good, the bearded, the white. Before you, Nocturnal Raccoon and I have pronounced headstrong words and disrespected your authority."

"Rise, Yellow Bird," I said to him. "I am aware of the punishment that befell you, and it pains me. The spirits are furious and have told me that, night after night, they will haunt both your tribe and Nocturnal Raccoon's."

"Take pity on us!" shouted the entire village. "Take pity on us, O Kukulkan, O Wise Owl!"

"Take pity on us!" wept Yellow Bird. "Take pity on us! Lift this terrible plague and we'll do anything you say!"

"I'll have a word with the spirits," I told them; and I went into my hut, closing the door. I took my flute and called for Good Sun, but a low-ranking mosquito came instead.

"Good Sun is indisposed," he told me, "and cannot come see

you. He begs your pardon and says he will come tonight for the blood."

"Very well," I said.

As soon as the mosquito left, I heard a great commotion and calls for death outside. I went out immediately and saw that Nocturnal Raccoon's entire tribe had just arrived, and that the wrath of Yellow Bird's tribe was falling upon them in the form of branches and stones. My presence alone was enough to quiet everyone down. Nocturnal Raccoon fell to his knees before me, weeping and lamenting:

"Wise Owl, Kukulkan, endless clouds of mosquitoes descended upon my tribe last night, drinking our blood and stealing off with our dreams! We can't live like this anymore!"

His entire tribe wept with him and lamented, the women wringing their hands and the men letting their tears stream freely down their faces. Yellow Bird's tribe immediately joined their weeping and resumed their pleading. Standing in my doorway, I felt I had gained the high ground and took advantage of my position to speak to them:

"Yellow Bird, Nocturnal Raccoon, all my friends. You have disobeyed the voices of the good spirits who speak through my mouth, and you have suffered the consequences. I can summon those spirits and secure you their forgiveness, but you must follow my orders."

"We'll do anything you say," several of them cried.

"You must join together in a single tribe, and accept my decision of who will be chief."

"You be our chief!" one man shouted, and all approved.

"No," I told them. "I will only give you counsel as a friend. Yellow Bird will be your chief."

Nocturnal Raccoon lowered his head in resignation.

"Yellow Bird will be your chief and, upon his death, you will decide his successor. In order to choose, you will all gather together, and after burying the dead chief, see who is most worthy of leading you. Then, you will elect and respect him. And if you do not do it this way, the plague you saw last night will descend upon you once again."

In silence, they all accepted what I had said. Nocturnal Raccoon offered to bring all his people with their houses and furnishings that very day.

"For now," I told them, "to calm the spirits and offer them something other than your blood, you will come out, every night until I tell you otherwise, wound a deer without killing it, and bring it here before my home, making sure to let fresh blood run from its wound, but not to let it die, and this you will do every night until I tell you otherwise."

All nodding, they scattered back to their various activities. I left my hut and went off in search of Good Sun.

IX

I walked deep into the jungle, calling out with my flute to any mosquito that might hear me. I knew that every time I made my way through the trees, several squadrons were flying behind me and ahead of me, so I trusted some captain would hear me and come talk to me. Finally, one appeared.

"It's urgent that I see Good Sun," I told him. "I need to see him right now."

"He is occupied with the Supreme Council," he answered, "but I will call for him. Wait on the small beach where you usually talk with him, and I will do as you wish."

The mosquito left and I headed for the place he had indicated. After waiting a few minutes, Good Sun appeared and said:

"I have been looking for you, as well. The Supreme Council has concluded its deliberations and sent several messengers to speak with you to keep you informed of their resolutions."

"Before we begin, I want to tell you something," I told him. "You punished my friends the Lacandon harshly ..."

"I warned you that the attack would be terrible," he replied.

"Yes," I answered him. "And I don't blame you for it, since I gave my consent. But now I have another idea. I saw the ease with which your suppliers sucked the wounded deer's blood. Every night, you will have a fresh deer before the door of my home, so you can take its blood."

"Last night, the deer caused you such pain," he said, a touch mockingly.

"The Lacandon cause me more."

"Fine: tonight we will come for the blood—but don't forget, or we will have to take it from your friends."

"I have something else to tell you," I said. "As it turns out, those Lacandon who live in the caribal four leagues away have moved here, too, so both tribes can live together and be close to me—"

"I see," he interrupted. "You don't want us to bother them either. Don't worry: so long as we receive our blood, we will not touch your friends. Now report back to your home and hear what the recordkeepers of the Supreme Council have to tell you."

I set out for my hut and found it full of mosquitoes. Almost all the Lacandon were waiting for me outside, and I had to send them away with the promise that if they brought me the wounded deer, as I had instructed, neither the mosquitoes nor the evil spirits would torment them again. Yellow Bird told me he wanted a few sheets of paper to make little boats and cast them off on the river, so the evil spirits would float away in them. I handed him some pages, and everyone left.

As soon as I walked into my hut, one of the recordkeepers came forward to tell me:

"Hear the word of the Supreme Council, the word entrusted to me! Greetings to the man who has learned our language and submitted himself to our will. So said the Supreme Council, one hour and thirty-five minutes ago."

"Hear the word of the Supreme Council," said another, "the word entrusted to me! The man who has learned our language must speak to us, the members of the Supreme Council, on this day, at night, in the location indicated to him. Good Sun, head of Logic at the Metasboc Corpus, which has summoned us, has been nominated to determine this location. So said the Supreme Council, one hour and sixteen minutes ago."

The recordkeepers fell silent, and I understood the moment had come in which I was supposed to speak; so, taking out my flute, I said:

"Greetings to the Supreme Council. I have heard your words

and will report to the place indicated to me, at the chosen time."

Immediately a number of recordkeepers began repeating my words, and they all flew off, leaving me alone. I could hear nothing more than the quiet hum of my security detail outside.

It was already late in the afternoon when Good Sun arrived, with several recordkeepers in tow.

"Human," he said to me, "as soon as night falls, you must report to the boulder on the shore of the lake north of the beach. And you must go alone—"

"Yes, I know. The recordkeepers already—"

"Listen, and do not interrupt me. You will report there and stand facing the lake until your name is pronounced, at which point you will turn around and listen to what the Supreme Council has to tell you. You may look at them, but you must not move, and speak only when asked a question."

"Okay," I said. "But I don't see any reason for such mystery and fuss, seeing as you and I are friends, Good Sun—"

"Fathoming these mysteries is no concern of yours. Many years ago, the Supreme and High Councils weighed every option and saw what must be done. Your only responsibility is to obey."

And having said this, he flew off without the customary salutation. I was left deep in thought. My friends the mosquitoes weren't my friends, after all: they were my masters, and they gave me orders. Under these conditions, reaching an agreement for a treaty with mankind seemed difficult to me. Maybe the best thing was not to show up at the meeting, and show them that you can't play games with a human. And after all, when all was said and done, what did I care if a truce were struck between humans and mosquitoes? Was anyone going to thank me for it? People forget favors quickly, that much was clear. No, I had no intention of working on behalf of the human race at large: I was interested in studying the organization and life of mosquitoes, writing a book about it, making money, and helping my friends the Lacandon.

The best way to achieve my goal was to attend the meeting with the Supreme Council and find out as much as possible, even if I didn't plan to accept their proposals. I couldn't miss this chance to see things no human had ever seen before.

Night was falling when I left my hut for the meeting place. I noticed the caribal was empty, surely because my friends the Lacandon were out hunting the deer I had requested. Walking along the shore of the lake, pushing through the many vines and lianas in my way, I made it to the beach, crossed it quickly, then sank back into the jungle. It was almost dark out, but I could see swarms of mosquitoes flying behind me and ahead of me, scaring all the animals out of my way. I walked about a half mile through the jungle and arrived at last at the foot of the rock they had indicated. I stopped there, looking out over the water. A massive swarm of mosquitoes had formed over its surface, dwarfing any I had ever seen before. Layer upon layer hovered mutely in the air, almost completely still. I heard the buzzing and voices of another mass behind me, but I remained still, as I had been instructed, facing the water. Among the mosquitoes hovering in the air above the lake, I noticed some large ones I had never seen before and other tiny ones, also unfamiliar to me. Little by little, after lengthy inspection, I realized there was a definite order among them, and that they were arranged according to their ranks. The bottom layer was composed of the suppliers I knew so well; the scouts were above them; next came the recordkeepers, whom I watched in silence for the first time. On top of these were the egg-layers, and above them, the army. Then came the logicians—among them, no doubt, my friend Good Sun. The following layer contained those large mosquitoes I knew nothing about, and, at the very top, those tiny ones. Suddenly the swarm set into motion and approached the shore until it towered over me, a single yard away. I had my flute pressed to my lips and thought of speaking to them, but something about the complete hush that had fallen over the jungle, something suffocating and terrible, forced me to remain silent. I noticed the entire jungle had become perfectly still: the birds no longer cried out in search of their nests, no crawling thing rustled over the ground—not a leaf trembled, not a monkey shrieked: nothing but suffocating silence. And for the first time I felt afraid, felt the desire to run. I took a step to my right and the swarm swelled to block my exit. The same happened when I stepped to my left, and I saw I had no choice but to stand still. Behind me, the clipped noises and buzzes began again— when, suddenly, a clear buzzing ordered me:

"Turn toward us, human."

X

As soon as the buzzing ended, I turned around and stood with my back to the lake, facing the great bushy jungle, over which towered an immense mahogany and a ruddy gumbo-limbo tree. At first I saw nothing, just an impenetrable black mass, constellated with unmoving white spots like eyes peering out at me. Little by little my vision adjusted to the dark and I realized that this enormous black mass was composed of large mosquitoes with a handful of white ones scattered among them. One began to buzz:

"Human who has learned our language, we are going to speak to you. We are the ones who think, and we have already thought of everything in the world. First and foremost, we want you to remain completely still and silent until you are instructed to speak. Do you understand?"

"Yes," I answered.

"Good. Now, listen closely, so these words may never escape your memory and you may preserve them forever. As soon as you proved that you had learned our language, the Metasboc Corpus, which governs their territory, notified all other corpora we maintain throughout the world; and so we have convened here in a Supreme Council, which represents two hundred eighty-three thousand five hundred twenty-four corpora, that is, nearly the totality of all extant corpora. Those who have not come are unimportant: they live in cold zones and are underdeveloped. From what I have just said, you should grasp the importance of this Supreme Council and obey its orders faithfully. Do you understand?"

"Yes," I answered again, although I didn't like this business about the orders very much.

"Good!" continued the mosquito who was speaking. "We will now inform you of the Supreme Council's decisions. All of this was already considered long ago, and we have simply heard the different opinions of the corpora—no more, no less. We have summarized our points so your human intelligence, with its little training, can understand them more easily. This is what we want to tell you: we are the supreme masters of the Universe and all its creatures must pay us tribute with the blood we mosquitoes require to live. You are already familiar with our societal organization and aware of our need for blood. All animals, to greater or lesser extents, have submitted to us and we use them as we see fit, granting them a partial freedom they consider absolute. As long as they pay us our tribute, we don't interfere in their internal affairs; this is true of all animals, except you humans, who, either because you are more advanced than the rest of the animals or simply more prideful, choose not to pay us our blood tribute peacefully, but instead invent methods to kill us and start minor wars. Do you understand?"

"Yes," I answered him. "And in these minor wars—as in Panama, as well as other places—you have been defeated."

"We have never been defeated. Some of our corpora have merely withdrawn in anticipation of the great moment you neither can nor should be aware of; but in that great moment the combat will be such that, if we so desire, no memory of the human race will remain at all. Now, this is not in our best interest. Humans have good blood that serves us well, and so we are willing, now that you have learned our language, to offer you a treaty of political alliance and friendship. Its clauses are easy to remember and we want you to relay them to mankind. First: humans will stop using, immediately and forever, the weapons you commercialize with the absurd purpose of killing us. Second: humans will understand that they owe us a blood tribute and will pay it accordingly. Third: in order to pay it, you will station a predetermined number of members of your species in locations of our choosing, for a definite amount of time, and these locations will constantly host three million individuals, who will be left unclothed and who will not interfere with the extraction of any and all blood we deem necessary. Fourth: mankind will not enter other sites of our choosing, for any reason, under penalty of death. Fifth: under no circumstances will a human kill any mosquito, and any human who does so will be placed in a location of our choosing and entirely drained of blood. These are our conditions. In exchange, we offer humanity not to transmit diseases to mankind, not to bother you in any location beyond those we have indicated, and to protect you against any animal that wishes to attack you. What do you say to this, human?"

"I find it unlikely," I began, "that mankind will accept those conditions. First, we have the problem that humans consider themselves the masters of the world and rate you among the inferior species. There is also the problem that they will simply refuse to pay this tribute. Please keep in mind that the human is creation's most intelligent animal—"

"So you think!" he interrupted me. "But I believe I have demonstrated to you that we mosquitoes are the most intelligent. We have achieved the greatest number of advances. We have successfully dispersed our cells in order to occupy many spaces at once—"

"That may be true," I broke in. "But you have lost the ability to procreate and cannot conceive a new body."

"We have no need of that. We have divided up the world and we are satisfied: see how little we are asking. There are more than two billion individual humans, and we are asking for only three million to satisfy our need for blood. Moreover, those three million individuals will not die but will be replaced by others once they are weak. Compared to our sacrifice of an infinite number of suppliers—"

"The case is not the same," I interrupted him. "You sacrifice no more than the cells of your body, which are easily replaced, but among us every person is a complete being, with intelligence, memory, initiative, will. Each and every human is like an entire corpus of yours, over which the rest can't or shouldn't exert more than a limited influence, because all men are fundamentally equal to one another—"

"Among you humans," he interrupted me, "some have power while others do not. Surely, the powerful can force the powerless to pay the blood tribute. Power is a grand thing to you humans, and you fight desperately over it because you have not achieved our level of perfection, at which it is entirely distributed."

"That level of perfection," I said, "has its downsides."

"And what might those be?" he asked, a bit sardonically.

"Your organization is so perfect that you have no initiative left. Everything goes to protecting your organization and securing food sources without ever imagining anything new, because everything has already been thought and you don't know how to think anymore. You only know how to summarize and give a twist to those old thoughts."

"An intriguing hypothesis," he replied, "and yet it has the defect of advocating for anarchy. If we have already discovered the perfect way of life, why would we change it?"

"That way of life may be perfect for the cells that make up your brain, which in your case are the mosquitoes of the council, but it isn't perfect for the rest of you; and maybe they'll want to change someday, if they begin to feel the need to be free, as humans once did."

"Nonsense. Why would the suppliers want to be free? They don't have enough brains to think: they're equipped only with what's necessary for carrying out our orders. But let's get back to human-mosquito relations. It appears you didn't like our proposals, and yet they are all profoundly just, since we are by far the more powerful and we could wipe man off the face of the earth with great ease. You claim humans are mutually independent, that each is self-sufficient. But that is exactly what would make you so vulnerable and easy to destroy—if we so chose. We have to restructure your organization and give you one similar to our own."

"That's impossible," I told him. "Nobody would allow himself to sink to the abject level of the suppliers. I have already told you, all men are created equal—"

"And I have already told you, that is clearly not true. But let's not belabor the point. We have already thought too much, and we are tired from doing so. You may go."

The black cloud at the foot of the mahogany tree disappeared in the blink of an eye, and the swarm over the lake behind me dissolved as if by enchantment. I walked slowly home to my hut and found Yellow Bird there at my door with a wounded deer dripping with blood. I told him to leave it on the ground and go home, without turning back. He had only just left when I found myself in a swarm of suppliers, and the terrible scene from the night before repeated itself. I had to reopen the deer's wound three times, following Good Sun's orders. I was leaning over it, when one of the suppliers whispered to me, pleading:

"Do you really think that there is hope for us, like you told the council? Could we really make something more of ourselves?"

I was going to answer her, when Good Sun interrupted us, reprimanding the supplier for wasting time on the job. And she quickly flew off to deliver the blood—the life—that she was carrying.

Once they had all left, I put the deer out of its misery, went into my hut, and started thinking.

XI

The following afternoon, I received another message from the Supreme Council, ordering me to a meeting at the same location. This time Good Sun did not deliver the message, nor was he present at any point, which got me thinking. Did the pride of these mosquitoes need to be broken? How could they possibly think they were on a par with humans? The more I thought about it, the more absurd it seemed to me—although, on the other hand, the mosquitoes also must have found it absurd that humans considered themselves their equals. Maybe it would help to understand something about their spiritual life. Did they have a soul like our own, did they believe in God, did they know Him like we do, or had they never achieved such knowledge by way of faith or reason? I realized the councils or brains had already thought of every possible future, and placed themselves in all imaginable situations; but I never saw them try to associate the past with the future, or try to understand cause and effect.

I thought of these things on my way to our meeting place, where the scene of the day before played out again. I believe it was the same mosquito who spoke to me; his voice, at least, sounded similar to me.

"Human," he said. "Have you considered last night's proposal?"

"Yes, I have considered it and regret to inform you that the humans cannot accept it. The only points we can accept are those concerned with putting an end to our war, since the spirit of peace always inspires human decision-making—"

"So," he interjected, "that's why you are always at war with each other."

"That," I said, "is another matter entirely."

"We ourselves lived that way, in the very distant past. By now we have evolved, and such pointless wars have ended. Now, go on."

"I'm telling you, we cannot accept it. We can neither consider ourselves your taxpayers, nor give you this blood you have so often demanded. Perhaps we could, in exchange for your friendship, give you blood from the animals we sacrifice for our own sustenance, and agree on certain ones that—"

"We did not ask you," he interrupted, "to propose new terms. We only want to know if you accept the duty of informing the humans of what we offered you last night. We will help make the people believe you; you can teach our language to a number of them, and convince them—"

"There's no point," I said. "The humans would never accept it."

"And you give us your answer without consulting them? Are you authorized to speak on behalf of all of mankind?"

"I'm not authorized, but I know that they will laugh in my face if I bring them this proposal. Humans aren't afraid of you and have weapons to destroy you."

"Think carefully. Is that your final decision?"

"Yes."

"Well then, we are left with only two options, both of which are based on the use of force. One of them consists in the prompt extermination of all humans. For that, we have the germs of diseases we have never used beyond mere experimentation, and which are foolproof. The other option is to violently subdue humans and govern them ourselves, as you do with your livestock. For this, we would need you."

"But," I interrupted. "I don't—"

"Silence! Don't open your mouth until we tell you to. You have already heard the two ways we can solve the human problem and

69

we believe the second is easiest for everyone. If asked to choose between slavery and death, many claim to prefer death, but in general slavery is preferable, above all the kind we would impose, which would be relatively light: we don't intend to destroy the entire human race, which we can make use of, just as you don't kill off all your livestock because a single animal might one day hurt or kill a man. We have learned, from what you have told Good Sun, that many men claim to prefer death, that your poets sing the praises of the few who have died in the pursuit of liberty; but we also know the majority of humans already live in a kind of slavery, often much harsher than the kind we would impose. Keep in mind that wealth and poverty would come to an end under our regime, since we would feed and clothe all equally, limiting the population to what can be properly maintained in each region. To do this, we need a human government to assist us. And this is where you, human, can be of use to us—and you must. Know that we would make you the most powerful human on earth, that all others would be subject to your command and will. You would have the right to decide whether they live or die, and we would provide you with an impenetrable security detail to protect you against any attempts on your person. Consider that, human."

And so I considered it. Now I see I should have reacted in some other way, the way the hero of a novel or a saint would have reacted, but I neither was nor am either of those things. I was just a man lost in the jungle, a man disowned by his family, a man who felt humiliated and reviled. I had never received anything but pain from society. In an instant, images from those forty years of bitterness, sadness, and humiliation flashed before my eyes, and I felt an intense hatred rising up to my throat and filling my entire being. That was my chance! Today, I could be the greatest man alive, so great they would never forget me as they always forget great men! What did I care if my reign were over slaves? I would be the most powerful man on earth—my revenge would be perfect, absolute.

As I was thinking all this over, a horrible, almost palpable silence fell over the jungle. The millions of mosquitoes around me stopped moving, so still that not even the air stirred, and all the animals grew quiet. Standing before the black cloud that draped the trunk of the mahogany, I thought these great thoughts of vengeance, and my soul felt charged with the immense anxiety of creation, of beginning anew. Finally, I spoke:

"I have weighed your reasons and understand them. It is clear you have thought of everything and have prepared a response to every possible circumstance. I am ready to help you dominate mankind so that some among them can be saved and the species doesn't seem—"

"Don't try to trick us or yourself with empty words," the mosquito interrupted me. "You know perfectly well that you have accepted because we have offered you complete control over mankind—just like the human you are, you desire power with all your might."

"It's true," I said, ashamed. "You speak the truth, but there's more to it. I don't love humanity—it has offered me nothing but insults and humiliation—and that's why I've agreed to serve you. I want to dominate humanity and change their way of life to a more just one, in which they all enjoy a certain equality—"

"They will," the mosquito who was speaking interrupted me. "They will enjoy the very same equality your livestock enjoy among you. And now that you have accepted our offer, as we were sure you would, given the benefits our plan will offer your species, we will now elaborate. The plan, outlined broadly many thousands of years ago, is divided into two stages. The first, which is temporary, is the war we will wage on humans in order to subdue them. For that, we will rely on countless elements. Once our program is ready, we will order the preparation of more than one hundred million soldier mosquitoes to spread diseases, among which we will include some mankind already knows, according to your conversations with Good Sun, such as yellow fever, malaria, sleeping sickness, and river blindness, as well as other minor ailments that manifest as rashes. In addition, we have others at our disposal that mankind is unaware of. A number of them are stored away in reserves we have used only in certain experimental cases, and which I would rather not explain to you now. But to give you an example, I will simply tell you about one of them. In certain zones, we keep special microbes that, when injected under human skin by our soldiers' needles, take only a few hours to cause an enormous blister, which grows to cover the entire body in two days, at which point the human dies in excruciating pain.

"We believe the war could last for up to two years, at the end of which, through your mediation, mankind will surrender. Then, we will carry out the second part of our program.

"No human food—except for sugar, which we will collect in great quantities—is of any use to us until it has been processed and converted into blood. The humans will perform this labor, and we will keep alive only as many humans as we have need of. The rest will be destroyed. The ones we let live, based on their strength and superior health, will labor eleven months of the year, producing food for their fellow humans and sugar for us, and during the remaining month they will go to locations of our choosing so we can suck their blood. All women capable of bearing children will be responsible for bearing more, and the women who are too old, along with all useless elderly men, will be killed without fail, so as not to waste vital provisions.

"In order to govern mankind, we will appoint a number of you, who will be exempt from the blood tax and enjoy our protection. You will be the first great governor; you alone, for now, will be exempt from tax or tribute. When you die, we will appoint another. You will be able to appoint all the representatives you consider necessary, but these posts will not liberate them from the tribute. Only you will be free from it—"

"But," I interrupted, "you had promised me that my friends the Lacandon would be exempt."

"Indeed, they will be free of tribute as long as they live. We have given our word and we know how to keep it. But such a favor will be granted to no other human being on earth, except the one who governs all others. Naturally, we will maintain a robust army to keep mankind in submission, but we will not infect the ones we use to produce blood, except for the few who will serve as live breeding grounds for germs, or as mobile arsenals.

"Once this has been achieved, we will be able to extend our corpora wherever we want, having secured the necessary food. Our only task will be to keep mankind under control, for which a moderately sized army and good microbial armaments will more than suffice. Any attempt at rebellion will be harshly put down, and we will kill without mercy anyone who has taken part and all who live in the surrounding area.

"Humans, as we understand it, have enjoyed many comforts they will have to do without, in order to focus entirely on producing food. We will only permit rudimentary sugar factories—all others will be destroyed. All men who know how to run factories, scientists, artists, as you call them, men who operate machinery, will be killed. We want humans to be nothing more than farmers, so that's what they will be. Do you understand?"

"Yes," I replied, alarmed by the magnitude of the project. "I understand."

"Well then, think over everything that will be necessary to carry out this plan, and communicate the results of your thinking to the members of this council who will stay here to discuss all necessary matters with you. I only want to say, our laws are rigorous and all who violate any aspect of them, however minor, are executed immediately and summarily."

As soon as the mosquito had said this, the immense black cloud vanished, and the lake cleared of the swarm of mosquitoes covering it.

Slowly, I headed for my hut to prepare the deer Yellow Bird had surely left behind. I should have walked away feeling satisfied—I was soon to be the most powerful man in the world—but something weighed on my heart.

When I arrived at my hut, there was Yellow Bird with his wounded deer.

"You must already know, O Quetzalcóatl! of the news I bring."

"Tell me," I said. "Tell me, in the way you understand it."

"Men of your race are making their way through the jungle. They do not come cutting timber or seeking gum. They come showing holy cards and looking into our lives. What should we do, O divine Kukulkan, O plumed serpent!"

I guessed immediately that it must be some scientific expedition, come in search of the Lacandon to study their lives and customs.

At that moment the presence of this expedition wasn't in my best interest at all, as it might interfere with my discussions and arrangements with the mosquitoes. So I asked Yellow Bird if they were close.

"No, they are still a day's journey away, if they walk straight toward us."

"Then leave tomorrow with all your people, and erase all traces and footsteps so they can't find us. They mustn't see us—if they do, the evil spirits could get angry with you, just like they did two nights ago."

I could tell my order didn't please Yellow Bird very much, but he had to accept it for fear of the mosquitoes, and he assented. Afraid this might be a trick, I said:

"If the white men making their way through the jungle find us here, you will no longer be chief and the evil spirits will rain a plague of mosquitoes down upon you that will cost you your life."

Bowing repeatedly, he returned to his village and I set about providing the necessary blood. Several suppliers buzzed secretly in my ear, while Good Sun was busy with other things:

"Do you really think there's hope for us? Do you really think we could stop being slaves if we wanted to?"

I didn't dare answer, for fear that Good Sun might overhear and hand me over to the council.

XII

Good Sun arrived at my hut before sunrise with several other mosquitoes. Among them were two of those white ones I had seen in the black mass under the mahogany and many of the tiny ones I saw hovering over the lake. Good Sun informed me this was the commission the Supreme Council had appointed to help me devise the plan of attack on humanity. The white mosquitoes were Supreme Council representatives and kept informed the messengers who, traversing the entire globe, carried messages between the High Councils. The tiny ones were Great Treasury accountants. The rest were mere recordkeepers and logicians. Good Sun began to speak:

"Human," he said to me, "the Supreme Council, whose name mustn't be pronounced, has selected these mosquitoes in my company as the commission. Posthaste and with your input, we want to devise a strategy for perfect combat to achieve the goals laid out for you last night, which you have accepted. Look, you have a friend in this mosquito—white as the air he flies; his name is Swift Wind, and he can tell us the capacities of every corpus across the globe. This other, smaller comrade is responsible for memorizing the accounts of all the corpora's treasuries and arsenals; his name is Infinite Memory. Each of them, as you can see, is accompanied by his consultants, and there are enough recordkeepers here to ensure that what we say will be remembered forever. And with that, let's begin our deliberations as soon as possible."

"Let's start right away," I said, thinking about how the white men were making their way through the jungle and how, despite Yellow Bird's speed, they might find us at any moment. Neither their presence nor their potential realization that the Lacandon considered me a god was in my interest.

We set to work right away and started organizing our plan, which the recordkeepers repeated in endless, unbroken whispers. To begin, we calculated the forces we had at our disposal, and I informed them of the humans' resources for battle. Given that mankind's principal resource is oil, we resolved that our first objective was to seize the oil fields. Without oil, society would already essentially be paralyzed; even so, we still thought it would be worthwhile to destroy the electric plants, railways, and seaports. To achieve such destruction, squadrons of mosquitoes would be deployed with bacteria to kill every human working in these zones.

With the world thus paralyzed—although of course we wouldn't interfere with the fields or farmers—we figured it would be simple to impose our conditions for peace and to focus on reorganizing society according to our vision.

The majority of the mosquito corpora are located near the equator, between thirty degrees latitude north and south, so the attacks would begin at the equator itself, moving north and south simultaneously. Each mosquito corpus would seek out a pool of water in some convenient location to incubate several million soldier larvae and the bacteria necessary to arm them. Meanwhile, in the usual locations, millions of egg-layers would be incubated and groomed to lay roughly one hundred million eggs per corpus, per day. The accountants said this would all be easy to organize and would require no more than twenty-five days of preparation.

While the battles were underway, I would wait in some location with a telegraph, or, if possible, a radio, to announce to the world the news of its enslavement and the new government that awaited it. We would set up the international military headquarters somewhere near to me, in order to receive all updates from the many attacks being waged around the world.

The corpora deep in the Amazon rain forest, and other places almost completely devoid of humans, would raise a great quantity of soldiers and the bacteria they would eventually carry, and would serve as reserves in case the humans managed to destroy any corpora during the struggle, however unlikely this might be.

We spent the whole day developing these plans and interrupted our work only when Yellow Bird called my name outside. I was able to give him the good news that we wouldn't be needing a wounded deer that night, since I had managed to calm the evil spirits with my pleas. He told me the white men were closer now and walking straight toward the village, even though the tribe had wiped away all footprints and traces of the camp. According to him, the white men already knew of the village and were looking expressly for it. I sent him away as best I could, ordering him not to speak with the people who were arriving until I told him to. I lingered a moment in my doorway, meditating on what I would do with my friends the Lacandon once I had become the leader of the entire world. Perhaps it would be best to place them as bosses of the groups of farmers, above all the farmers of my own race, so the latter might finally understand what it means to feel humiliated and despised—although, of course, they would have felt this quite clearly already when they became the mosquitoes' slaves.

When I walked back into my hut, we continued drawing up our plans. To incubate enough bacteria for our program, we would need a reliable source of fresh blood, so we decided that every corpus should capture a number of men to take their blood and use them as live arsenals of nonlethal bacteria. That was when I learned the mosquitoes can, if they so desire, relieve humans of bacteria by injecting them with antitoxins, and that they had already done this with me, to relieve my malarial fever. Once we wrapped up this point, we moved on to the question of the world's organization after we had won the war.

For now, each corpus would maintain a zone where no human was allowed to enter under penalty of death. Around these zones, in which the treasuries and High Council residences would be kept, another zone would be designated for the humans who were to serve as the corpora's food source. The necessary quantity of humans would be calculated according to each corpus's size. The other humans, meanwhile, would work in the fields, producing food for themselves and sugar for the mosquitoes. Of course, with their food so readily assured, every corpus would grow a great deal, even coming to fill their entire territory, and the number of humans permitted on earth would be decided in accordance with the mosquitoes' needs.

In cold climates little fit for the mosquitoes, special zones would be established, with areas dedicated to human reproduction, which would be perfectly controlled so there would never be more humans than necessary. Through crossbreeding, they would attempt to create a strong race of good blood, but of the lowest intellectual capacity possible, so as to prevent a human uprising that could force the mosquitoes to exterminate the species. Naturally, there would be no schools or anything of the sort; writing would be lost and the arts would come to an end, along with everything currently known as culture.

The humans would be allowed livestock, houses, a specific garment of leather and crude fabric, fire, and rudimentary agricultural tools, but all factories would be closed and destroyed, the railroads would be razed, the use of petroleum, electric light, and every class of weapon prohibited. They would be divided into classes. One pool, the producers of blood for bacteria, would have to remain in the indicated areas surrounding each High Council until they died of the illness injected into them. Another branch would be the manual workers, who would dedicate twelve hours a day to agricultural tasks and the production of everything necessary to feed both themselves and the mosquitoes. Another subset of men, and all young women, would be set aside for reproduction. Lastly, some would be assigned to the management and organization of all this. Regardless of their physical condition, all older men and women were to be killed as soon as they turned fifty, with the exception of those serving in government.

Any man who, for any reason, killed a mosquito, avoided his labor, disobeyed orders, entered a prohibited area, or attempted to invent any instrument to engage the mosquitoes in combat, would be summarily executed. Death was the only punishment, and it would be doled out without exception.

Once we had developed this plan, the two large mosquitoes, with the help of certain messengers they kept on hand, set about presenting it to every corpus in the world, to see if there were any objections.

We spent two days on this, two days I spent in revery, imagining myself on top of the world, lord and master of all life and fortune. I recall this moment like a dream full of ideas, ambitions, and longings. They were the greatest days of my life.

On the third day, early in the morning, someone knocked on the door of my hut; I answered in Maya that they could come in, and the door opened, making way for a man and woman of my race. He must have been around fifty, with a bushy blond beard, beady, inquisitive eyes, and thinning gray hair. He wore white riding pants, tall boots, an open shirt, and a white cork helmet. A pair of pince-nez spectacles hung from a ribbon around his neck. The woman was young, probably about thirty, with a fine, intelligent face; her body, tall and slim, was no stranger to exercise.

The man addressed me in Spanish:

"The name's Wassell, Professor Wassell. The Indians refused to speak to us and directed me to your home."

"Pleased to meet you," I answered. I asked him to come in, and did the same with the young lady.

"This is my secretary, Ms. Johnes," the man replied as he entered my hut. The woman followed him in. I sat on my hammock and looked up expectantly, waiting for them to inform me of the purpose of their visit. It was the man who continued speaking. The woman had hardly smiled once, and had not spoken at all.

"We've come for the Lacandon Indians—to study them and see what possibilities might exist for incorporating them into civil society. We've been commissioned by the federal and state governments. In San Quintín they told us we might find you here, although nobody knew your name."

"Around here, they call me Wise Owl," I replied.

The woman finally cracked a smile, but the professor kept talking.

"None of the Indians wanted to talk to us, no matter how hard our interpreters tried to start a conversation with them. One of our guides told me he found evidence that the paths and footsteps had been wiped away, to prevent us from finding the village. Now, why might they have done this?"

"Because I told them to," I replied. "We don't want any intrusions here from the evil known as civilization. And consider yourselves warned: should you so much as think of giving alcohol to the tribe, or showing it to them, or drinking in their presence, I will kill you."

Now the woman was watching me with interest. The professor rose sedately.

"We didn't come here to get Indians drunk," he said sharply. "Naturally, we brought some bottles for our crew and—"

"In that case, I ask that you hand them over immediately, so I can destroy them. If you don't, your journey will have been a waste of time, because I will order the tribes not to speak to you, and they will obey me."

"Sir, I am a representative of the Government..."

"As far as I can tell," I replied slowly, "any government is one government too many. I'm the government here—I'm the law, the three branches or however many branches I damn well see fit to be. So, now that we understand each other, if you don't like it, you can leave."

The professor rose and left my hut with dignity. The woman, sitting on the table with her feet dangling in the air, kept looking at me with something between a smile and admiration on her face. It looked as if she might say something, but suddenly she hopped down to the floor and followed the professor out. I lingered in the doorway to see where they were going. They headed for the village, and nearby I saw the other members of the caravan: lumberjacks and cargo carriers and other men wearing helmets.

XIII

Good Sun informed me that several messengers had returned and that all the corpora had approved our plan, setting the date for the beginning of the war at the start of the rainy season. It was January, so we had at least four months to get everything ready. Our corpus, as well as some others in the zones of Chiapas and Tabasco, had been assigned to attack the Minatitlán oil fields and paralyze the railroads and port. Next, we would have to transfer our larva treasuries to some favorable location along the Coat-zacoalcos River and advance north, until we had completely de-populated Veracruz, and join with the northern corpora waging war on Tampico and that entire oil-rich area. Once united, we would advance to the Mesa Central to attack the big cities.

Similar attacks would be taking place simultaneously in all countries within the tropics, and we figured that once these had been taken we could dictate our conditions to every human on earth. If they refused to accept, we would let winter pass, occupy-ing the northern- and southernmost posts with our treasuries and arsenals prepared to attack the northern countries come spring, and bringing live arsenals along with us, if it proved necessary. The final target of all corpora fighting along our route was New York in July of the coming year. Within the territory of the United States there are several mosquito corpora, but they are neither rich nor powerful, so they would require backup. While we waged our first battles, those corpora would focus entirely on expanding their treasuries and arsenals, in order to be ready with the largest reserve possible when the time came. Some corpora along the Mississippi River claimed that they would be able to destroy certain cities and oil fields unassisted, namely the port of New Orleans, but this was not approved, for fear that, given their weakness, they could be defeated, giving the humans time to study beforehand the bacteria we planned to infect them with.

In order to prevent the humans from defending themselves with insecticide, the mosquitoes engineered a type of mask for their soldiers to wear. The mask was made of a resinous fluid they secreted naturally, but I wasn't entirely sold on its effectiveness. It had been tested with good results, but only as protection against the smoke used by the Lacandon. To test it against real insecticides we decided to steal a small dose of the strongest insecticide from the expedition that had just arrived, and to perform experiments on a number of our soldiers.

I left my hut in the afternoon and walked up to the caribal. The members of the expedition did not greet me, but Yellow Bird came forward enthusiastically, bowing deeply. He didn't wait to tell me that he wasn't responsible for the arrival of the white men, that he had followed all my orders and hadn't said a word.

The crew members had set up their tents beside the caribal. I eyed them all, but didn't see the professor or Ms. Johnes anywhere, so I figured they must be inside one of the tents.

"Go," I told Yellow Bird, "and tell the chief of the white men that I am waiting to have a word with him in my hut. And that the woman should come with him, too."

Yellow Bird went toward one of the tents and I to my hut. I don't know why I thought to order the woman to come too, but I took a certain pleasure in talking to her, seeing her, feeling the admiration I aroused in her.

A few moments later, Professor Wassell arrived with his secretary. As soon as he walked in I noticed he was carrying a concealed pistol under his light white coat; it appeared the woman had seen me take notice of it, and that she was laughing at him just a little.

"The tribal chief told me," the professor began, "you would like to speak with me. I suppose you've thought things over and would like to change your opinion on how to proceed ..."

"Not exactly," I said. "I still insist you hand over all the alcohol you have in your possession before interacting with the Lacandon."

"I don't understand your attitude, Mr. ..." the professor said, trying to draw out my name. But it still wasn't in my best interest for him to know it, so I said:

"In these parts, they call me Wise Owl. As for my other name: I have forgotten it, and don't care to remember it."

"All right, well, whatever your name is, I'm telling you I don't understand your attitude. We are only trying to carry out a scientific mission. I have come as a member of the Carnegie Institute with two other colleagues, one of whom is a philologist and the other a great musician who hopes to compile the music of these peoples. Ms. Johnes has come as our secretary, and Ms. López is a representative of the state government. Beyond that, we brought along a few guides and porters."

"That's all good and well," I interjected. "I have nothing against you performing whatever studies you like, although I'm afraid they'll be of little use. All I ask is that you hand over all the alcohol you brought, and any insecticide you have."

"Our insecticide!" cried the professor. "You must be out of your mind, Mr. ... Wise Owl."

The woman smiled almost imperceptibly—I may have been the only one to notice she had laughed.

"There are no mosquitoes here. You won't be needing any insecticide," I told him. "I, however, may need some for a certain experiment I'm performing."

"You're a researcher, too?" the woman asked.

"Yes, ma'am," I answered her. "But my research is concerned with matters none of you would understand. I study mosquitoes."

"Interesting," interrupted the professor. "Very interesting, indeed! I know a bit of zoology, myself, and thought I might perform a few studies—"

"Not with me you won't," I retorted sharply. "Or perhaps we will perform some together, after all," I added, with a new idea popping into my head. "Perhaps you and your crew could help me a great deal with my experiments."

"I'd be delighted!" the professor nearly shouted. "I had no idea you were a researcher. Please count us in, but in exchange for our help with your experiments, I would like you to allow us to—"

"Once I have all your alcohol in my possession," I replied, "you'll be able to talk to the tribes and do whatever you want, although I'm afraid you're only wasting your time ..."

The woman laughed again, but with a smug, conceited laugh that rubbed me the wrong way. The professor reflected, and finally said:

"Good thinking, Mr. ... hmm ... Mr. Wise Owl. After all, I don't really see any problem in our handing over the bottles we've got, as long as you promise to keep them in case one of us were to catch some illness that requires—"

"Accepted," I told him. "I will put your bottles in safekeeping."

The professor rose and walked out, promising to send all the bottles in his camp immediately. The woman lingered behind, sitting on the table, watching me with a peculiar smile. When the door had closed behind her boss, she said:

"Tell me, Wise Owl, what do you mean when you say our research will be a waste of time?"

"Those are things that only I know," I replied, "but which shouldn't be of any concern to you."

"I don't see why our research wouldn't be of any use. I think this expedition will prove to be of great benefit: the tribes who live in this area will be better understood ..."

"Yes, they may be better understood, but it's already too late."

"Why's that?"

"Well ... because it's always too late to understand things."

"And you say this because you think these tribes are going to disappear?"

"Maybe," I answered. "Or maybe because I think everything humans do is useless ..."

"And even so, you continue your research."

"Yes, I do my research—but on more serious matters."

The woman looked at me, laughing rather sardonically. So I was forced to tell her:

"What I research is so serious that the entire future of humanity may very well depend on it."

"Oh, really, now?" she said, still grinning.

"Yes," I replied. "My research is the only worthwhile thing happening in the world right now. Someday you'll find out what I'm researching, and you won't be laughing at me anymore—"

"Oh, I don't mean to laugh at you," she interrupted. "I just find you very interesting is all, Sir Mr. Wise Owl, and I think our points of view overlap on many things."

"On what? You know nothing about me—not what I think or what I'm planning to do."

"That's true, I don't know any of that. But I've been watching you. It must be pretty fun to turn yourself into a god overnight, even if it's only for a handful of savages."

"Excuse me? I have no idea what you're talking about," I answered, making an astonished face, but also understanding, with a certain vague fear, that she had already figured out the nature of my relationship with the Lacandon.

"For a god, you strike me as understanding very little, Mr. Wise Owl. But please, excuse me, I'm going to the river to see if I can't find a place to take a dip."

And having said this, she stepped out of my hut. I was left alone to brood. I wanted to think about my future power, but, somehow or other, I always ended up picturing Ms. Johnes and coming up with all sorts of snappy comebacks that would be sure to put an end to that laughter of hers.

While I was lost in all these thoughts, two expedition men walked in with a number of boxes full of bottles. I told the men to put them down in a corner, and they went off to bring me all the insecticide from their camp. And so they left, promising to come back with what I had asked for, but not without shooting a few curious glances at the table where Yellow Bird's gods were laid out. As soon as I was alone, I called for Good Sun. He was perched on my rooftop and came right away.

"I have the insecticide to test the masks," I told him. "It would be best if you brought several soldiers and had them put on their masks, so we could test them as soon as possible."

Almost at the same time as the two crew members returned, carrying a spray pump and two containers of commercial insecticide, Good Sun flew back in, followed by a hundred or so soldiers with their masks already on. I filled the canister and ordered the soldiers to position themselves in front of me. Then I instructed the mosquitoes there to oversee the experiment to place themselves behind me, afraid I might kill them as well . . .

The soldiers all gathered in a stuffy corner with little airflow, and I started to spritz them with the insecticide. Once I had saturated the air, I set down the pump and stepped back, joining the mosquitoes awaiting the experiment's results. Two or three of the soldiers fell suddenly to the ground, but the others kept hovering there. I picked up the cadavers of those three and put them down in front of Good Sun, so he could examine them.

"These masks are poorly manufactured," he told me, "and the gas got in. That's why they died, and it's what they deserve for their carelessness. I will order that their names be forgotten forever."

The other soldiers in the experiment seemed to be doing fine, and Good Sun ordered them to fly forward. One of them said:

"We didn't feel the situation to be lethal, but we believe that in order for these masks to be perfected we will need them to cover the entire body, because the liquid burns our skin terribly on contact, and I think we would die if there were too much of it."

"Go to the arsenal," Good Sun answered, "and perform the necessary tests."

At that moment, the door opened and Ms. Johnes walked in. I still had my flute pressed to my lips.

"I forgot to ask you if it's dangerous to go swimming in the river," she said once she was inside. "But I see you like music. I'll be sure to tell Mr. Godínez, the expedition's musicologist."

"You can swim in the river as much as you like, as long as you don't stray too far from the shore," I replied. "But no, I'm not fond of music, nor do I have time for such child's play. This flute is part of my research."

Apparently my snappy tone didn't affect her at all. She made herself right at home and sat down at the table.

"I really do find you incredibly interesting, Mr. Wise Owl," she told me. "You weaseled all of Dr. Wassell's insecticide out of him by claiming it was unnecessary, and here I find you spraying it profusely in your own home. Is this also part of your research?"

"It is, in fact. And I ask you to leave me alone now—I have a long day of work ahead of me."

Without moving, she simply laughed.

"And all this time I thought that the charm of becoming a god lay precisely in not needing to work. You know, Sir Owl, I heard some members of the tribe saying that you are Kukulkan or Quetzalcóatl of the Nahuas, and that really piqued my interest."

"They have no idea what they're talking about," I answered angrily. "Just because I've done them a few trivial favors, they've taken me for a god—"

"Your mistake was that you forgot to tell them otherwise, wasn't it? Or perhaps you've done well..."

"What do you mean?"

"By not telling them otherwise. Not just anyone gets to become a god. Besides, the tribes told me you liberated them from evil spirits—"

"Well now, I see that they've spoken with you quite a bit."

"Not the men, but the women are easy. I just go into their houses and ask them for something or other and start chatting. One of them told me you freed them from the mosquitoes ..."

I looked down without answering. It wouldn't have been good to start in on that dangerous subject before everything was in place. She continued, as if amused by my embarrassment:

"She says that whenever you play your flute you're summoning the evil spirits and the good ones, too, and that you ordered the mosquitoes to stop bothering the tribe. Well, I thought that was pretty amazing, but now I see it's not your flute but insecticide that you use to scare off the mosquitoes, which takes away a great deal of your charm. But seeing as you're not amused by my conversation, I'm going to go off for my dip in the river."

For a moment I felt a strange urge to hold her back, but I let her leave without a word. I don't know why, but I, I who have forgotten so many things, perfectly recall every single word she said to me and the punishments I suffered as I took them in, one by one.

XIV

All through the night, I thought about my conversation with Ms. Johnes, and suddenly I understood that the presence of white men had once again disturbed my peace. I felt an uncontrollable desire to try the liquor lying in wait for me in the corner of my hut, but the fear of starting all over again paralyzed me in my hammock. I suddenly realized that in my mad dash for supreme power over men, I had stopped hating them as I had before, in the days when their injustices drove me to squander my life away in the inviting jungles. But now, faced with such people again, I felt this hatred and an unprecedented desire for revenge rising up once more, which gave me the strength to go on with the plan we had already laid out.

"The whole world is in my hands," I thought. "I am the master of everything man possesses on the face of this earth: his things, his lives—his women."

But as I began to think of women, the image of Ms. Johnes came back to me—that sardonic woman, who seemed to laugh at everything I said, but then sought out my company.

I got up before sunrise and walked outside to sit by the river. Maybe if I had reached out for help in that regretful moment, these tragedies could have been avoided. Maybe I should have followed the path of God, but at that point, so close to my great power, I didn't believe in God. He had created man and made him lord and master of the world, lord and master of all creation; but I was going to use my power to destroy the very idea of God and to debase man, His most perfect creation, to the status of livestock bought and sold at the market. Thinking this way, of course, it was impossible to believe in God, a God unknown to the mosquitoes who were soon to become the masters of the world. Or was He really so unknown to them? I had never addressed that point with Good Sun, and it was probably better that way. I didn't even know the word in Mosquil for God.

But if God did exist, He was not going to allow mankind to be wiped off the face of the earth before the inevitable moment had arrived, as He had conceived it. Or perhaps, grown weary of man's evils once again, he was going to use the unconscious mosquitoes and myself—my vanity, my pride, and my resentment—to punish man and force him back onto the path of goodness, toward complete salvation.

In that moment, sitting by the river, I knew I shouldn't be thinking of those things, yet they came to mind against my will: they assaulted me, and I felt an indescribable fear, a fear at once vague and concrete, before God. And so I tried to reassure myself, repeating to myself that He didn't exist, that the world was the product of random coincidence, and I can't say how many other pieces of nonsense inspired by the pseudo-philosophical books I'd read in my youth. But if the world had truly been produced by coincidence, then this placed the power to topple the dominant order and create another squarely in my powerful hands, in my intelligence. So I was nothing more than a blind force of coincidence; and this gave me the strength to rebel, and it made my soul tremble with pride. It had been nice to be a pawn in the chess set of an intelligent God, of a powerful creator deity; but even better was what my mother had taught me: to be a free entity, even before a creator deity, the God who had created us in His image and likeness. And yet, if this were true, if my mother's unblemished faith were correct—however vehemently I had rejected it, and for however long—then I was not only betraying the human race, but also God, the God who had created me; and I was selling out my soul in exchange for such power over slaves.

That morning, I think, was the closest I came to regret. The power I was going to acquire no longer looked so beautiful or sweet when I saw it through the Lord. I remember that, just for a moment, I was on the verge of getting up to find Professor Wassell and asking him to take me far away from this jungle, far from these awful temptations. But then I heard voices behind me and, when I turned around, I saw one of the crew members—later I learned this was Godínez, the musician—chatting with Ms. Johnes and walking to the river with his arm around her. Quickly I hid in the scrub, watching them as they sat down in the very place I had just been sitting and, leaning their heads together, chatted on.

Then, overcome again by an anger I couldn't fully comprehend, I forged the final, most perverse stage of the plan: once the world had been conquered, man would be forbidden all contact with God, all religion. I was going to have to explain the necessity of this measure to the Supreme Council. The council had to understand the dangers posed to our plans by any communication between God and humanity, because that godly imperative turns man into a strong and free being, something which had to be avoided at all costs.

Good Sun buzzed his salutation in my ear. Picking up my flute, which I always carried around my neck, I answered him, unveiling this new article we would have to incorporate into our plan for subduing mankind.

"The Supreme Being?" he said, repeating the term I had used to convey my idea to him. "I have never heard of such a thing; I don't know what you're referring to."

"Humans," I explained, "believe in God, the Supreme Being who created them and gave them everything they have. Above all, humans believe this God gave them the freedom to think, to work, and to choose between good and evil."

"Now I understand," he said. "God is the human's High Council."

"No, God is above both the High and Supreme Councils. God is infinite, and all-powerful. God created every mosquito and human out of nothing—"

"I don't follow," he interrupted, "but if you want me to, I will relay your words to the representatives of the Supreme Council, whose name mustn't be pronounced—perhaps they will understand you better. But if you think that humanity's belief in this thing you speak of could hinder our plans in any way, we will snuff it out."

"As long as they believe in God, men will never truly be slaves," I replied. "He is freedom's strongest foundation, and taking away that belief won't be as easy as you think."

"Everything is possible," he told me. "I will bring your words before the council, and they will already have made a decision about it."

No sooner had Good Sun left than a supplier approached and buzzed in my ear.

"I heard what you said," she told me, "and I have also listened to other words of yours, which you pronounced before the Unnameable. I want you to explain to me why humans are free and why we, the suppliers and the scouts, are not. If God created all of us, we must all be free."

"Yes," I replied, "you could all be free if you believed in God, if you had a God, but not even I believe in Him anymore."

"Why not?"

"Because, well . . . for personal reasons."

"But if the High Council believes in God, then we should believe in God, too," she told me. "We believe everything that the High Council believes, but it has never spoken to us of God, nor have we heard the recordkeepers mention such a thing. If the High Council knew, surely they would have mentioned it before. But farewell for now, I have to go suck blood from those two humans on the beach."

Ms. Johnes and Godínez had gotten up and were walking slowly upstream, along the entire beach. She had let him take her hand in his, and they were speaking in whispers, as lovers do. I remained hidden among the scrub, lingering behind them, without knowing why.

Some Lacandon children arrived at the riverbank and saw me right away, for what remains hidden in the jungle for people of my race sits in plain sight for the Lacandon. After greeting me with deep bows, they asked me for sheets of paper. Instead of just giving them some, I emerged from my hiding place and made them little boats and played with them, creating such a stir that Ms. Johnes turned her head and saw us, which is exactly what I was hoping for. She approached us with her companion and gazed awhile at the little boats and the children playing with them in the water. Then, with a smile, as always, she said to me:

"I don't believe you've met Mr. Godínez. He's our expedition's musicologist. Mr. Godínez, Mr. Wise Owl."

We shook hands, but I noticed she had taken on a sarcastic tone, probably to point out to her friend the hilarity of the name I had been given, but which she used because she didn't know any other. Godínez also appeared to regard me with a certain degree of mockery. The young woman spoke first:

"So you're casting away the evil spirits, I see," she said. "One of the Indian women told me about this stupendous system of yours for casting away evil."

"Those women seem to tell you many things," I told her. "It's only a game for the children—"

"Well, the adults have taken it very seriously."

"And how, exactly, am I responsible for that?" I shouted, almost angry now.

"You're not," she said, smiling, always smiling. "I just found it amusing."

Without answering, I withdrew to close myself away in my hut, where I could be alone and think. But it wasn't possible, because

Dr. Wassell came to introduce me to the rest of his crew and tell me they were about to begin their work. I was as amicable as possible; I showed them where I had stashed the liquor and sent them on their way. As soon as they left, Good Sun spoke to me:

"The representatives of the Supreme Council, whose name mustn't be pronounced, want to speak with you to discuss this new initiative of yours. They are awaiting you beside the mahogany tree, and it would be best for you to come with me."

Before initiating the discussions, the Supreme Council representatives dispatched all the mosquitoes in their company, ordering the soldiers to form a barrier around us so no one could interrupt our conversation.

"Good Sun," one of them told me, once we were safely alone, "delivered your message to us. We may find ourselves in grave danger because of you, but we won't hold you accountable, for you didn't know any better."

"I don't understand what you mean," I said.

"You have spoken of God," he told me. "And that is dangerous. We never speak of Him; the populace, the insignificant mosquitoes, must not even be aware of His existence, because it would jeopardize our entire organization."

"So then," I said, "you know of God."

"We do," answered the one who was speaking. "But the Supreme Council is alone in this knowledge, and never speaks of it. When we were still joined together in a single body, we duly worshipped Him. That was long before man appeared on earth. Now every corpus's High Council worships Him, but the dispersed cells are completely unaware of Him, and the recordkeepers do not record such words. If the suppliers, for example, were to discover the existence of God, they would consider themselves our equals and it would bring our perfect organization to an end."

"Now I understand," I told him. "Don't worry, I won't speak of it again."

"Excellent. As for mankind, it would be good to take any idea of God away from them. Of course, we will tell our subjects that humans believe in nonsense and tall tales. But you must not speak of this again."

"I most certainly will not," I answered. "But now I want to talk to you about another matter. Several men have arrived here, and I believe fortune has sent them our way. Thanks to them, we now have ideal live arsenals and enough blood to feed our germs and the members of the High Council while they develop our plans."

"That was our idea, too," said the one who was speaking. "And we will make it so."

"I believe it would be best to take them prisoner, since they are planning to stay only a short time," I told them, "and for this we will need to put our power on display, but I will have to speak to them beforehand. It may be necessary to kill one or two of them, but the ones left behind will be more than enough for our purposes."

"Do as you wish, and we will send Good Sun. He will provide you with inoculants and all other necessary materials, but don't let them leave this site, and most importantly, don't allow any of them to be alone once you have spoken to them: the moment for the human world to learn of our plans is yet to come."

"That's just what I will do," I said.

With that, I bid farewell to the representatives and withdrew to my hut to think over the new plan that had occurred to me. Ms. Johnes wouldn't be laughing anymore.

She came to visit me that night, when the sun had already set. As always, she was smiling and seemed to feel right at home. She came in without asking and sat herself down on my hammock, rocking slowly back and forth while she looked at me. I pretended not to notice, but watched her out of the corner of my eye. She was wearing a white skirt and a light blouse; she wasn't wearing stockings, just a pair of strange huaraches. Her blonde hair fell over her shoulders as if uncombed, but I could tell how much effort she had put into making exactly that impression, and I felt a certain pleasure imagining that she had prepared her whole look just to please me. But why would this woman want to please me? And besides, what did I care if she thought about me at all? I was busy with bigger things, things so big she'd never be able to understand or imagine them.

Suddenly, she said to me:

"The Indians told me you talk to the mosquitoes with that extraordinary flute of yours."

For a moment, I didn't know what to say. Then I mustered:

"They have no idea what they're talking about. Who has ever been able to talk to an insect?"

"You know, Mr. Owl—"

"Don't call me that," I interrupted. "I do have a real name, after all."

"Well, I don't know it, and besides, you yourself asked me to call you that."

"That's what I told Professor Wassell, but you should call me by my real name."

And so I told her my name, but she only laughed and told me she liked Wise Owl better.

"You know," she continued. "I've read lots of mystery novels. Maybe that's why I see mysteries everywhere—and you strike me as a mystery. For starters: what are you even doing here? You're not one of those Indian exploiters, and I haven't seen you making any efforts to find gold or precious wood. In the civilized world, you could really be making something of yourself—"

"That's what I used to think!" I shouted.

"But you didn't have the strength to stand up to the world, and you let it get the best of you, so you came here to hide your disappointment away in the middle of this godforsaken jungle."

"That's the story, more or less," I answered. I don't know what drove me to speak; but something inside me was forcing me to recount all my hatred, malice, and pain to this woman. Maybe she could understand me—maybe she could even save me. "That's the story," I repeated, "the whole vulgar story. As you say, I could have made something of myself, and I will yet, something far greater than anything I could have ever dreamt before. But for this to be possible, I have had to walk the paths of rancor and spite—"

"Don't you see how right I am?" she broke in, laughing. "There really is something mysterious about you—and mysteries simply fascinate me."

I don't know why her interruption bothered me, but I sat back down at the table and opened my notebook again. I had finally decided to open my heart to a person of my race, thinking she would understand me; but that stupid interruption slammed the door in my face and left me emptier than ever before. She kept prattling on, completely unaware of what she had done.

"Antonio, Mr. Godínez, will be coming for me any moment now. He invited me for a walk on the beach, for lack of anything else to do."

"And so," I asked, "why exactly did you come to my house? Why didn't you leave camp with him?"

"Professor Wassell has certain aspirations for me. I would hate to offend him."

"So you go around with the musician on the sly."

"Not on the sly," she answered back, becoming serious. "But I still don't want the professor to find out that Mr. Godínez and I are engaged. I really do care and have so much respect for the professor, and I would feel just awful if he were to get upset. I want to get the idea in his head little by little that I'm not going to marry him. But none of this must be very interesting to you. I came to your house because I like your mysterious way of talking. As I said, I—"

"And are you thinking of marrying Godínez?"

"Yes," she answered. "We'll be getting married as soon as we make it back to civilization. Do you think we'll be happy together, Mr. Owl?"

I didn't answer her question. I can't remember what I was thinking at that moment, but I do remember that my heart hurt, thanks again to the cruelty of mankind. That beautiful, cheerful woman was deceiving the professor and making a fool out of me. The world was the same as it had always been: humans were beyond salvation. They would have to be annihilated or so thoroughly dominated that they would live like livestock forevermore. Only then would they walk the straight path. Only as slaves of a superior species could they be freed of the burden of their evil.

But Godínez's entrance cut my meditations short. He hardly greeted me at all, striding immediately to Ms. Johnes's side.

"Let's go," she said, standing up.

And I was left alone, with a newfound spite. But how could the future master of the world feel spite? I put my thoughts aside and started thinking over my plan to take the expedition into our custody.

XV

I called for Professor Wassell early in the morning, ordering him to report to my hut with his entire crew because I needed to speak with them. When they arrived I seated them as best I could, and sat down facing them behind my table. Ms. Johnes tried to sit at the table, too, but I asked her to sit with the rest. She did so without argument, but looked at me curiously and, as always, with a smile.

"She won't be smiling for long," I thought.

Once everyone was seated, the expedition heads up front and the chicleros in the back, I began my speech in a slow, clear voice, so that all present would understand me perfectly—later, we wouldn't have any misunderstandings.

"Ladies and gentlemen," I said to them, "I have often told you—Dr. Wassell and Ms. Johnes in particular, who are both here with us now—that I am conducting an extremely important experiment, perhaps the most important one ever undertaken. Ms. Johnes has laughed at me endlessly, and it seems to me that Dr. Wassell has doubted my capacity as a researcher—"

"Oh, no!" the professor exclaimed. "I never—"

"Don't interrupt me," I said. "Now, I believe the time has come to tell you about my experiments, and to ask you to help me carry them out to their happy conclusion."

"We are absolutely ready," the professor interrupted again. "Just the other day, I told you that we would be glad to cooperate with you on your research, but since I don't have even the remotest idea of what it's about, I haven't been able—"

"And now you're going to find out. In short, I have learned the language of the mosquitoes. Please, do not interrupt," I rushed to add, seeing that several men in the room were making to speak. "Yes, I have learned the language of the mosquitoes, the language spoken by every mosquito in the world, and by means of this language I have communicated with them, so much so that I have perfected my knowledge of their organization and lives. I believe, as you can imagine, that this is the first time such a thing has ever taken place in the history of the world: never before has a human being has been able to comprehend the language of one of the species we might consider irrational, and communicate with it."

A number of people—that Godínez, in particular—let out idiotic guffaws. I could already tell they weren't going to understand, and I didn't care. The important thing was that they come away with a clear grasp of the role they were going to play in the new world order, over which I would rule. In grueling detail I explained what would be expected of them, how they were not to leave this site, and the laws that would govern their lives from that day forth—which is to say, the laws that the mosquitoes would instate on our day of victory.

As I spoke, the professor began to look bored, Ms. Johnes watched me curiously, and the others appeared as interested as if they were listening to an entertaining story. But it was plain to see that they didn't believe a single word of what I said. And so I concluded, after speaking for two hours:

"Naturally, the scientific spirit of a number of you and the foolish skepticism of the rest will demand proof of what I have said. The proof will be terrible, but definitive. This very afternoon, a mosquito will bite Mr. Godínez, and within a few hours he will have died from a disease previously unknown to man. First, a blister will form at the location of the bite, then this blister will grow until it covers his entire body, and he will die in excruciating pain. This is the proof I can offer you."

"I think he's insane," said Ms. Johnes.

"My proof is irrefutable," I argued. "Once Mr. Godínez has died—"

"And how can we be sure he died from a disease given to him by a mosquito?" Ms. Johnes asked. "It would be easy for you to slip him some poisonous herb that causes symptoms like the ones you just described—"

"One moment, please," I interrupted. "I want the proof I offer to be scientific, achieved under completely controlled circumstances. To be sure of this, I ask that the subject of the experiment lock himself up in his hut and eat only food he himself prepares, in order to rule out this possibility of poisoning that Ms. Johnes has suggested. Professor Wassell, and anyone else who cares to, can stay in the hut with Mr. Godínez, to watch over him and make sure this is no trick. A huge amount of mosquitoes will show up in his tent tonight, but they will bite only the subject of the experiment, so the rest of those present need not take any precautions. The subject may take whatever precautions he likes, but I tell you here and now that they will be useless, because both the mosquitoes and I have decided that Mr. Godínez must die—we are determined to experiment on this new disease with his body, and Mr. Godínez will inevitably die."

"Let's get out of here," said Ms. Johnes, standing up and interrupting me. "This Wise Owl is much crazier than we thought. Mr. Godínez, come with me to the river; let's go see if we can't find a nice spot for a swim. Good afternoon, Sir Owl, your talk has been more than entertaining, but it's gone on for too long."

And so Ms. Johnes left my hut, followed by Godínez. Professor Wassell watched them for a moment, as if thinking of following them, but his expression changed, and he remained seated, lost in thought. I could see clearly that he was thinking much more about Ms. Johnes and Mr. Godínez than about the marvelous experiment I had just laid out before his eyes. This confirmed my opinion of mankind's pettiness and misery. To awaken him from his meditations, I said quietly: "Such a shame Mr. Godínez has to die, isn't it? Ms. Johnes is going to be devastated, being his fiancée and all."

The professor looked up, but saw nothing; his eyes were blank. Slowly he stood and left my hut, heading for camp. The others dispersed without a word.

Good Sun hovered beside me, and I told him everything that had happened, though without going into detail on the romantic conflicts between the professor and Mr. Godínez. I'm not sure why, but the whole time I spoke to him my eyes were searching for the silver of riverbank through the doorway, though I couldn't see a thing.

"What are we going to do, then?" asked Good Sun. "From what you've said, these men are the very finest human scientists and they don't believe what you've told them. The rest of the species are even less likely to believe you."

"We'll simply have to show them," I answered. "That's why I foretold Mr. Godínez's death. I want a huge squadron of soldiers and females to gather tonight with the disease we discussed and to take care of biting Mr. Godínez, whom I have already pointed out to you. They mustn't bite anyone else, because that would undermine my proof. They must bite him and only him, making sure to inject him with the bacteria—and he must die without fail within the time frame I specified."

"Very well," he told me. "I'll go make the preparations."

"Once Mr. Godínez has died," I continued, "or once he is so sick that all of human science isn't enough to cure him, I want to make those people another display, for which I'll need several mosquito squadrons at my disposal. Then they'll see that none of them can leave the premises without facing immediate death. But your soldiers must also clearly understand they are forbidden from trying to kill any more of those humans . . ."

"They are well aware. The High Council and the Supreme Council have stated that any mosquito responsible for the death of any of these humans without an express order from the High Council will be summarily executed."

"Excellent," I told him. "We'll need to keep these people alive if we are going to use them in our war. Now, go and make the necessary preparations."

Good Sun disappeared and I wandered out of my hut in no particular direction, but my footsteps led me to the riverbank. I scanned the whole beach with my eyes. At one end, under a blanket they had propped up to block the sun, Ms. Johnes and Godínez were reclined, speaking in whispers, her head upon his shoulder. I needed to know what they were planning, so I sank back into the scrub, and very carefully approached them without drawing their attention. I sat myself down under a bay cedar and started to listen.

Yet they weren't saying anything about what I had told them, nothing of his death drawing so near: they spoke of love and of their life to come. To avoid making noise, I was unable to leave, and I was forced to listen—for an entire hour—to the stubborn words that flowed from their hearts. Finally, they stood up to go, and I was able to withdraw.

Back at camp, no white man was to be seen. The professor, they told me, was shut away studying in his tent. His assistants had gone out on a hunt with the chicleros and guides. Yellow Bird came out to talk to me, bowing deeply.

"O great Kukulkan! Wise Owl!" he said to me. "These white men are good, for they have given us none of the liquor in which they hide evil spirits, but white blankets and colorful ones and knives and axes instead, and they don't ask us to work in exchange for them. They only want us to sing and speak to them while they make a black circle spin."

"Yes," I told him, "they are good, and that's why I've allowed them to stay here, and they are going to stay forever, and you, Yellow Bird, are going to be their chief and the chief of many great tribes. This I promise you, and, as you have seen, my words never fail to come true."

"Thank you, O Kukulkan! You have brought goodness among us and my words cannot express to you the joy that is in my heart and in the hearts of the men and women of my tribes. But I want to tell you one thing. There is a deep sadness in the heart of the chief of the white men, for he cannot buy the blonde woman who left with the other man. If you are his friend, you must help him buy her, because his heart is withering away in solitude and his soul suffers profoundly. If you want, we can buy her with good, strong runá wood, because there is much of it in the jungle, and with rubber, too."

"How do you know that?" I asked him.

"The chicleros talk at night around the bonfires, and many of them speak in Maya, and I heard them myself. I have also seen the white chief's sadness and how his eyes seek the woman, with the look of a puppy watching out for its mother."

"We will have to think more on this," I told him. "Maybe we can do something."

"But O Kukulkan!" he added, "forgive the audacity of my words, for I know well I cannot advise you. Yet I have also seen desire in your eyes. I have thought of it in the night, and I have said to myself: He must not desire her, for if he desired her she would be his, and she would go to his home and sit at his feet upon the floor and listen to his words, for he is Kukulkan—he who can do anything. But now I say to myself: If you desire her, bring her to your home, and my entire tribe will chop down trees and harvest rubber to pay for her."

"I know you would, Yellow Bird: I know it in my heart, and with my heart I thank you; but I do not desire her."

I saw my words saddened him and that he did not believe

them, but he didn't dare talk back. I didn't feel good about what I had said. I probably should have told him that the gods don't desire mortal women, or something like that. But it was too late.

I walked to my hut and tried to focus my thoughts on my future greatness, but Yellow Bird's words were spinning around my head: "If he desired her, she would go to his home and sit at his feet and listen to his words." But it was impossible for me to desire that: I was too great, too powerful a man to suffer over a woman, or even to desire one. A world of exalted opportunity blossomed before me: I would be the most powerful man on earth, the greatest and most feared king ... but "she would sit at my feet and listen to my words" and maybe I could run my fingers gently through her blonde hair as it fell over her shoulders. No, what mattered was the war—that perfect, unemotional organization. "The entire tribe would chop down mahoganies and harvest rubber to pay for her and make her your own." Mine, mine, sitting at my feet in the nights, listening to my every last word, drinking them in with her big blue eyes while I ran my fingers through her hair cascading down over her shoulders. But all men, of every climate, would obey me, would listen to my words—I would be the master of the world. And she would have to listen to my words, would have to know them, would have to sit at my feet ...

I don't know why, but delirium made these ideas spin in circles. At nightfall I left my hut and ran to the beach, but it was already empty. All that was left on the sand were the mark of where she had been sitting and the cigarette butt she had snuffed out, stabbing it into the wet dirt.

I washed my face and my hands and the cold water brought me back to my senses. Slowly, I walked back to my hut.

XVI

It was already late by the time Good Sun arrived. I was lying in my hammock, slowly fighting to regain my balance after the afternoon's extreme delirium.

"Everything is ready," he told me. "The squadrons have been armed and are already stationed in the enemy's quarters. Tomorrow we will see the results."

"Excellent," I said.

"I have ordered the recordkeepers to report back here and keep us abreast of what is happening, so we can expect them soon."

"In the meantime, let's talk," I suggested, afraid my strange delirium might return, afraid Ms. Johnes's image might keep appearing in my mind. And so we talked for a long time—I can't say for how many hours. I hardly replied to Good Sun at all, and my thoughts often wandered to things I didn't care to remember. This was my first night of greatness, the night when all my feelings should have been focused on the events around me. I should have been like Good Sun, speaking only of our future power and the war that was only just beginning. But I wasn't thinking about all that. Against my will, my brain insisted on bringing dead images back to life, and there appeared before my eyes my mother, gone for so many years now, and the sullen face of my father, who never quite knew how to raise me or lead me down the path he intended for me. And I saw my grandparents, especially that sweet little old lady who taught me the Christian doctrine when I was a boy in the corridor of her house, both of us sitting in the shade, she in her wicker chair and I on my little stool. And then, when we finished our lesson, she would hand me walnut candies and a few cents. I could still see her billowy dresses of matte-black satin, which I so loved to press against my face, just to hear the rustling fabric, and that little bag of hers where she kept her house keys, her prayer book, the handkerchief and sewing needles she never put down. Other times I helped her rinse camellia leaves and turn the soil in her pots, always bursting with flowers. And I knew that all the prettiest flowers from those pots were bound for her living room's altar to Our Lady, which she always kept closed—she cared for them with the very same devotion with which she assisted the elderly priest of her parish during mass.

But through all these images, Good Sun's constant buzzing and the monotonous, engulfing chant of the jungle filtered endlessly into my brain. And I saw the apparition of Ms. Johnes sitting at my feet, and I ran my fingers through her blonde hair as it cascaded over her shoulders and onto her back.

I wanted then to come back to reality and cling to the words Good Sun was buzzing and which I, with my flute, offered in return, but it was all useless.

That was the worst night of all those years—though, it should have been the greatest of my life: I knew it, I could feel it inside me. But instead of thinking about that, other thoughts hit me, thoughts I should have throttled years before, or which I never should have had at all, thoughts that rose anxiously to my throat and, squeezing my chest like a thousand-pound hand, robbed me of my joy over being strong and possessed of such power. Against my will, my lips began to whisper a prayer, the prayer my grandmother always repeated:

> *Sweet Mother, leave not my side,*
> *And look not away from me …*

But no matter how I tried, I couldn't remember the rest. The verses jammed and spun around my head, amidst all the other images and ideas tormenting me.

For a moment, as I recalled my grandmother, I thought of God, of that God in whom I scarcely believed, in whom the High Council mosquitoes believed but kept secret in order to control their subjects.

"What would happen," I wondered, "if I spoke of God to the less powerful mosquitoes, to the oppressed species?"

But I shouldn't have been thinking about that: I should have been thinking about the war so soon to be unleashed, the war that would bring me such power.

"Nothing exists outside of God," my grandmother had told me one day.

And if that were the case, my power, the immense power I was soon to take on in a matter of days, would exist within God. But that couldn't have been true: my power was against Him, was meant to strip all humans of their belief in God, because that belief prevented them from ever being truly enslaved. Godless men were easy prey—men such as myself. That's why I had made such easy prey for all those vices and misfortunes, that's why I had given in to bitterness and hatred.

"Nothing exists outside of God," my grandmother was telling me again, that poor little old lady who had lived in another world. But on that bitter night of my first triumph, I felt that something really did exist outside of God: my power, my strength.

A recordkeeper arrived with news:

"All squadrons have assumed their positions inside the tent of the indicated victim. A woman is with him."

"Don't touch her," I said.

"We won't touch her," he answered me. "We already attacked the victim, but he successfully defended himself and killed four comrades. Now, he has taken shelter inside a mosquito net—"

This one hadn't finished speaking, when another recordkeeper arrived.

"We've located a hole in the net, which a few soldiers can use to get in."

"Excellent," I told him. "Have them sneak in and attack him."

"They already did, but he continued to defend himself and killed three of the four comrades that got in."

"Have them attack in silence," I ordered. "The best would be for several to sneak in through the hole and, once they're inside, attack him all at once. That way it's ensured that at least one of them will be able to bite him. Give them those orders."

The mosquito said he would do so, and disappeared.

We fell silent for a long time, until the recordkeeper who had taken my orders returned.

"We carried out your orders," he told us. "Fifty or so comrades got in through the hole and attacked him all at once, in complete silence. The victim covered himself entirely with fabrics and defended himself desperately, but we knew he would have to expose his face to take a breath, and we took advantage of this to bite him. Three comrades succeeded in their attempt, but only half-way—he crushed them before they could finish. Then he called for help from the woman who was with him. She lifted the net and we used this opportunity to sneak in over two hundred more, who were able to bite and inject him repeatedly. The woman was fighting desperately, so I ordered a swarm of mosquitoes free of diseases to drive her away from the bed. They swarmed in front of her face, bit her, and tormented her, but she kept fighting in the man's defense. That's how I left them—still engaged in battle."

"Hurry!" I told him. "Tell them to withdraw. Mission accomplished—you mustn't continue tormenting them, especially not the woman."

The mosquito disappeared and came back a few minutes later to report that all his comrades had withdrawn after injecting enough bacteria into Godínez's bloodstream to assure his death.

It was almost four in the morning now and I decided to lie down, but I couldn't fall asleep. Those old thoughts continued tormenting me, spinning around my head in an insane procession of raving visions. The sun had only just begun to rise when I got up and went to bathe in the river. The cold water soothed my nerves, and I was able to think calmly again.

The first battle had been waged and won. Now it was time to use that victory to convince the expedition of what I had promised: we didn't want to be forced to kill them all, since we were going to need them as mobile arsenals. And we would appeal to science to predict all the symptoms of the disease Godínez was going to suffer and convince Professor Wassell. Once he was convinced, we would be able to bend them all to our will, having made it clear that their only other choice was death. Perhaps as a reward for good behavior, after we had won the war and taken control of the world, the mosquitoes could cure these humans of the diseases they themselves had incubated, and possibly even exempt them from the blood tax.

With these ideas in mind I went looking for Professor Wassell. I found him squatting against the trunk of a mahogany, smoking nervously. Without a greeting, I sat down by his side and looked at him. He clearly hadn't slept that night, either: his puffy eyes had black bags under them, and his hands were shaking. Yet I knew it wasn't thoughts of the human race's imminent destruction that had kept him awake, but his jealousy. I don't think he had noticed I was sitting there watching him, because when I spoke he jumped, like a man jolted awake from a dream:

"Sounds like Mr. Godínez had a long night," I told him

"Ms. Johnes and I talked last night. She's going to marry Mr. Godínez."

"Oh, she won't be getting married," I told him. "Mr. Godínez's body will soon be covered in one immense and excruciatingly painful blister, and by tomorrow he'll be dead."

"Back to your tall tales again," he told me. "I'm in no mood for them right now. Please, just leave me alone."

"Go to Godínez's tent and ask him what happened last night."

"I have nothing to ask Mr. Godínez," Professor Wassell answered. "That man and I have nothing to talk about."

There was a moment of silence, but on his face I could see the struggle taking place inside him—an unspoken, terrible struggle, the struggle of a pain that wants to break free and infuse everything, to rage against the education pushing it down to the very bottom of the soul. Finally, he looked at me from head to toe, as if studying me in detail. Then he lowered his eyes and began to speak:

"I mentored Godínez. I brought him along on this expedition. He was starving in the city: he's a pathetic hack of a musician and I felt so bad for him that I brought him along with us so he could earn some money and at least take home enough to eat. Ever since the first day, I felt like he was paying too much attention to Ms. Johnes, but I trusted her—I've known her since she was a girl. I knew her father, a professor of archaeology. Sure, I'm a bit older, but I can provide for her: money, respectability, a legitimate home. I told her all this last night, but nothing I said could make any difference. She's already made up her mind to marry that ... that hack ..."

"She won't be marrying him," I told him again. "Godínez will be dead by tomorrow night. He must already be feeling sick ..."

But Professor Wassell didn't seem to hear me. He was engulfed in his pain and anxiety, churning over his friend's betrayal and the loss of the woman he loved—there was no room for any other thought. I left him there and headed for Godínez's tent. I walked in without announcing my presence. The musician was splayed out on his bed and Ms. Johnes was cooling his forehead with a wet rag. She saw me first and paused momentarily, but a moan from the sick man's throat snapped her out of it, and she went on with her task. Once she had placed the rag on his forehead again, she stood up and approached me.

"He has a fever," she told me.

"I know. He'll be dead by tomorrow night. I warned you—remember?"

"You're out of your mind," she answered me. "It's impossible; it's insane, completely and utterly insane."

"It's the truth," I told her. "Professor Wassell has chosen not to believe me either: he's too preoccupied with his pain."

A mist of pity blew over her white face; her blue eyes clouded up, and as she spoke I thought I could hear tears trembling among her words:

"I had to say something. But if he dies, I'm dying too. I can't go on living, I can't ..."

The sick man called her name from his bed. From the faintness of his voice I could tell he was seriously ill, and I approached him without fear. A large blister had overtaken half his face and was slowly spreading. The woman set about gently rubbing salve over the blister and cooling his forehead, hot with fever. I left the tent in silence and walked back to the professor:

"Godínez is dying," I told him. "His face has already blistered over and he's running a terrible fever. I don't think he'll even make it until tomorrow night."

Wassell turned toward me. In his eyes I saw a new life, a hope—but that glimmer suddenly vanished. He was a man of science, after all, a strong and honorable man.

"What disease is it?" he said to me.

"It's unknown. This is the first time the mosquitoes have ever used it."

Without a word, he stood up and headed for Godínez's tent, from which he quickly emerged to go to his own and fetch a small briefcase—full of medicine, I supposed. I leaned against the trunk, taking it all in. Over in Yellow Bird's house, a number of children were chattering into a phonograph, while the elders looked on, in awe, at the scene.

XVII

Godínez died that day at dawn, died in excruciating pain, his entire body covered in one immense blister that had burst here and there, releasing a foul-smelling, viscous liquid. Ms. Johnes never left his side—she took care of him, with help from Professor Wassell and the other woman with the expedition, whose name I can't remember.

When I found out he had died, I asked Yellow Bird to build a coffin and dig a grave far away in the jungle. I also sent some children to go looking for flowers and bring them back to the tent—I hoped, in this way, to help alleviate Ms. Johnes's pain.

Good Sun came to see me, and I informed him the experiment had produced good results. That very afternoon, that very day, I said, I would persuade the members of the expedition that the best thing for them to do was to surrender. Good Sun looked pleased and flew off to bring my words before the High Council. I sat in my doorway and waited for the funeral to run its course, so that, afterward, I could talk to everyone and reach a definitive agreement.

But when the clock struck 3:00 p.m. there was still no sign that the ceremony had even begun, so I got up and made my way to the caribal. Nocturnal Raccoon came out to meet me with great displays of veneration, and I asked him why they weren't going ahead with the burial.

"The woman is weeping," he told me. "She doesn't want to leave the dead man's side, but he is already fragrant and needs to be buried."

"Go and tell them to bury him immediately."

Florentino Kimbol had followed his father and lingered behind as if he wanted to say something to me. To help him along, I said hello. He answered with his customary smile, and told me:

"I know the mosquitoes killed the white man."

"Perhaps," I answered him. "I wasn't aware."

"You could have stopped it, because you have power over the mosquitoes. Why didn't you stop it, O Wise Owl?"

"I protect only my friends, Florentino Kimbol, and the white men aren't my friends."

"You told them they're all going to die," he continued. "The chicleros speak in Maya at night beside the fire where they cook their meals, and I can understand what they say. They also say you're a madman and that the evil spirits have crept into your heart, but my father doesn't believe it, because you have been good to us . . ."

"And do you believe it?" I asked.

"No, I don't believe it."

Having said this, he went away, but I had seen the doubt in his eyes. I was about to follow him when the funeral procession appeared and I changed my mind. Four chicleros walked at the head, carrying the coffin. Ms. Johnes followed, clutching Professor Wassell's arm, and, behind them, the rest of the expedition, the men with their heads uncovered and the other woman in a veil. She walked along praying aloud, and the words sounded at once brand-new and ancient to my ears. She prayed the rosary, which some of the men intoned along with her in a whisper, as if half-heartedly. It all seemed to remind me of something, but the image wouldn't solidify in my mind—it slipped out of my grasp and hid in the wrinkles of the past. The funeral passed by in front of me and marched on. They all pretended not to see me. Some of the Lacandon went to join the procession, silently requesting my permission with their eyes. I signaled to them that they could go, and off they went, led by Yellow Bird and Nocturnal Raccoon.

I waited for them to return to the caribal, thinking about death. Even in the most remote places, people tend to shroud it with so much ceremony, always hoping to take away its power, but in the world to come, in the mosquitoes' new world, human death would take on about the same importance as the death of cattle in our city's slaughterhouses has today. In my opinion, this would remedy many of humanity's ills, such as pain and mourning. I do believe the image of Ms. Johnes, with her face covered, convulsing in tears, leaning on the professor's arm, treading weakly over the earth, moved me. And yet I already knew that all great works require pain, that all real changes in the world, every change that has led to good, such as Christianity, has laid its foundations upon blood and suffering. But was the change I had in mind actually going to lead to good? I had numbly formulated the theory that humanity could survive only if these changes were made, and I could no longer conceive of any other way of life. Without me, the mosquitoes' attack would wipe out the human race, so I had become its savior. And it wasn't a matter of saving a mere culture or idea: it was a matter of saving mankind's very existence, and the task had fallen to me—a task I was consciously lifting onto my own shoulders.

With such theories I had managed to quell my doubts; but now, faced with reality, they reawakened, clutching my throat and clenching my chest. It's one thing to think about pain in the abstract, and another to see it palpably before you, to see it in a woman's feet dragging themselves through the dust, which show that the woman's soul is also dragging itself along, that it has been emptied of hope, emptied of everything good in the world, and filled back up with nothing but pain and anguish.

Suddenly I felt someone's eyes on me and I turned my head. Florentino Kimbol, standing in the doorway of his house, was watching me attentively, as if studying me.

When I saw him, I said:

"I thought you were going to the funeral. Your father and Yellow Bird went. Why didn't you go?"

"I didn't want to," he told me. "My heart is sad."

"Why? You hardly knew the white man ..."

"It is not sad for any white man," he answered. "It is sad for my tribe."

We fell silent for a while. With downcast eyes, he was building little hills of dust with his bare feet. I saw him, saw his broad, blackened feet with their blunt toenails, when suddenly I thought about those other feet, those feet dragging themselves through the dust like symbols of human suffering, then about all the feet dragging themselves throughout the world, through that entire world that would soon be mine, those slow, afflicted feet stirring the loose soil, as if seeking hope within it, as if digging a furrow to sow the seed of this hope in it, but moving on without having placed a thing in that furrow, and moving on, slowly seeking something, anything, in this world.

Florentino Kimbol spoke:

"You too, O Wise Owl! You feel sadness in your heart, and there is no joy in your eyes when the children approach you."

"They are men of my race."

"The blonde woman is also of your race, and she chose the white man who has died."

"What makes you say that?"

"Because your heart desires to have her beside you. My father and Yellow Bird have spoken in the night, and they have conferred with Black Ant, who knows all things, and Black Ant told them that your heart desires her, for you are Kukulkan, the white and the good, and you are seeking a companion. But I know this can't be true, for the gods feel no desire since they possess everything. That is what a priest in San Quintín preached when I was there. He told us one day that God can do everything, that He had made everything and that everything belonged to Him."

"My heart does not desire her," I answered back.

Florentino's words had sprung up, fast and tremulous, like the words of a man who has long hesitated to say something and finally blurts it out.

"So then, why did you let them kill the white man?"

"That was his destiny."

"If you killed him because of the woman," he continued as if he hadn't heard my answer, "the tribe will be very sad. We have all trusted in you, we joined together because of you and dreamt great dreams because of you, and hope has taken its place in our village and we have welcomed it into our homes beside the fires we never let go out, because our gods never gave us anything, never told us anything, and you have spoken to us and we have found goodness in your words and our hearts have rejoiced. But the white man's arrival has brought sadness among us, and death has taken the place that hope once held in our homes. The blonde woman is the one who brought death here, and if you leave us—"

"I'm not thinking of going anywhere," I told him, to cut off, for even just a moment, that rush of words that were piercing me so deeply.

"There are many ways you could leave us," he told me, speaking more slowly now. "You could go away and never return, but you could also stay here and empty your thoughts of us in order to fill them with that woman. Either way we will be left alone, and the tribe will be saddened by your absence, and there will be much weeping, because we will look for you but we will not find you; and we have grown accustomed to you, to your good words and counsel. Yes, Wise Owl, my heart is telling me: the blonde woman will bring sorrow to our village."

And having said this, he disappeared into his home. I walked into my hut with sadness inside me.

That night, Good Sun spoke to me:

"The human we sentenced to death has died, and the High

Council wants to know what his companions have told you: if they are willing to obey us or if they prefer war, because if that is what they prefer, they will all die—one by one."

"I haven't been able to talk to them yet."

"You have done wrong. We have no time to waste. Nearly all of them have good blood. A few have malaria, and we will have to wait for them to recover before we begin, but the others have first-rate blood we can use to feed the High Council, especially that woman who visits your house."

"The woman?" I asked.

"Yes, the woman. In the meantime, it is imperative that you speak to them, so we can start our preparations. We will have to move the woman closer to keep the High Council fed; that way we'll be able to keep a greater number of females on hand to raise larvae."

"The woman's blood?" I asked again.

"Yes, as I just said, her blood is the best of all—the most potent. Only on very select occasions have we seen such blood. The High Council is quite pleased, and will be using it as its main food source during these days—"

"Be quiet!" I said sharply. "Don't say another word about that woman."

"I don't understand. I don't understand what's happened to you. Yesterday you were completely ready to—"

"Leave me alone," I demanded. "I will talk to them tomorrow, and you will have your way."

But Good Sun did not leave. Perched there on the rope that held up my hammock, he buzzed on and on. For a second, I thought about how easy it would be to crush him between my palms, but something froze me in my place. He was saying:

"I don't know what happened to you, but let me tell you. When we start something, whatever it is, it gets finished, no matter what: we are going ahead with our plan."

"I know," I said. "I'm just a little nervous tonight. I'll talk to them tomorrow, and everything will be arranged."

But Good Sun was not convinced, and he kept on talking. His buzzing became intolerable to me and I asked him to be quiet or leave. I don't know why, but the image of her feet dragging themselves over the loose earth came back to me endlessly, along with Florentino Kimbol's words: "The blonde woman will bring sorrow to our village." As always, the woman, the blonde woman, Ms. Johnes sitting at my feet, listening to my words: Ms. Johnes sobbing behind the mosquito net protecting her, Ms. Johnes dragging her feet over the loose earth; her, always her!

Desperate, I fled my hut and wandered through the moonlit jungle.

XVIII

By around nine in the morning everyone had already gathered outside my hut. Everyone except Ms. Johnes, that is. Yellow Bird had summoned them and, per my orders, they had come. The professor's face was inscrutable to me: it looked indifferent, dead. The others offered a variety of facial expressions: some looked curious, others bored, and others afraid—especially the chicleros. I stopped in front of them all, and said:

"One of you is missing. I want everyone present."

Nobody answered me, so I repeated myself. The professor, as if awakening from a dream, said:

"You will have to excuse Ms. Johnes. Her present state of health will not allow her to leave her tent. I gave her a morphine shot, and she is sleeping."

Having said this, his gaze was lost once again in the void, and I began my speech: "You have seen by now that I have told you no lies. A mosquito bit Mr. Godínez, and he's now dead. I imagine you are convinced and won't be needing further proof."

They all looked at each other in silence, but no one said a word. So I continued:

"Well then, as of this moment you are all slaves of the High Council of Mosquitoes and will follow my orders blindly. You're already familiar with the punishment for disobedience. Whoever disregards an order, kills a mosquito, or attempts to flee will be summarily executed—"

Professor Wassell stood up, shouting:

"Enough of your idiocy! Isn't all the pain you've caused us with this deranged sideshow of yours enough? Can't you stop torturing us and standing in our way? We don't believe a word of your stories. And as soon as Ms. Johnes is well, we'll be leaving this place—at the first outpost of civilization we find we plan to inform the authorities of what you're up to, and they'll be hearing all about how you've ruined our mission!"

"So," I asked him coldly, "you don't believe in the mosquitoes' power?"

"No," he answered me. "Why would I believe such tall tales?"

"And Mr. Godínez's death?"

"Let me tell you one thing, Mr. Wise Owl: I still haven't looked deeply into Mr. Godínez's death, but if I find out that you had a single thing to do with it, I will not wait for the authorities to handle it—I'll take the law into my own hands."

And having said this, he stalked off toward Ms. Johnes's tent. The rest of the expedition sat in silence before me, but slowly began to disperse, starting with the scientists and ending with the guides and chicleros. The proof I had offered through Godínez had fallen short—something else would be necessary.

Good Sun spoke to me:

"What happened? I saw how the tall man, the one you say is their chief, stormed off shouting ..."

I told him what had happened and how the professor had threatened my life. He promised to watch over me.

XIX

My heart was sad. All day I tried to sleep, but the bitter anxiety clutching my throat choked me. I kept remembering the liquor Professor Wassell had left in a corner of my hut … but I resisted the temptation and didn't touch it.

Good Sun came by many times in the afternoon. He told me that several mosquito squadrons were guarding me and that I had nothing to fear. But I wasn't afraid of what could come from the outside: I was afraid of what I carried within. Often I was assaulted by thoughts of God, but I did everything I possibly could to reject them. This was no time to think about God—it was a time to act, and yet I was not acting. I was lying in my hammock, letting the hours meander by, while outside, in the sunlit clearings and in the jungle's shadows, the future of the entire human race was at stake. And all the while, Ms. Johnes was sleeping in her tent and the professor was watching over her, seeing all, knowing all. But God couldn't exist, mustn't exist, even if the High Council believed in Him—even though I myself, deep in the tormented depths of my soul, believed in Him too.

A supplier flew up to me and said:

"We want you to repeat for us the things we've heard you say before. All of us suppliers are waiting—not for the war to be waged against humans, but for the moment of our liberation. What does it matter if the world belongs to us, if we still belong to the High Council and have no freedom to enjoy our lives?"

"Be quiet," I told her. "If a council member hears you, you'll be executed."

"Don't be afraid," she answered. "Many of the soldiers have the same ideas and we all know that we could be free if only someone helped us to think, because we aren't used to thinking ourselves. We have seen the other free animals in the jungle and we believe they worship the same God you sometimes mention to us. We want to be like them, even if we're not as strong."

The supplier's supplicant buzz, in its bright soprano range, reached my very soul. The mosquitoes wanted to be free, just like the humans I was going to enslave.

"We all trust you," she continued. "The squadrons of soldiers who have been stationed here to keep watch and guard you are outside, and they all want to follow your orders. We've even been able to bring some of the logicians over to our side—we can take the treasury and arsenal and then we'd be even stronger than the High Council. And if we can't take them, you can destroy them, because we know where you can find the—"

"Speak quietly," I told her again. "The die has been cast, and the war must first be waged against mankind. Then, we'll see."

"That's fine," she answered me. "But tell us just one thing. Tell me if God is real and if we are all equal under Him, the members of the Great Council and the suppliers—"

"Yes," I told her, "He is real. Now, go back to your duties." The supplier flew off and left me more confused than ever. If the mosquitoes wanted to be free, how could I want to enslave mankind? God would never allow it, but I couldn't let myself believe in God. And besides, all my dreams of power, of vengeance, of satisfying my hatred had to come true. Mankind was like Godínez, stealing the wife of the man who had helped him, the one who had given him bread. That was how all people were—like dogs, or worse—and there was nothing wrong with controlling and enslaving them. Surely humans were more perverse than the mosquito; and so the latter deserved to rule the world, and I deserved power over the former.

Whoever may be reading this must understand that these

words are neither an apology nor a plea for forgiveness. I put them down here only so what I have said may be better understood. I write them with death before me, and they are true because they are being squeezed from a heart ruined by fear and pain.

I heard footsteps outside my hut and went to the door to see who was coming. It was Professor Wassell, walking slowly, with his eyes fixed on mine, his hands stuffed in the pockets of his blazer. Over his head I saw a veritable swarm of mosquitoes, compact and dark. The sun was going down, but there was still enough light to see everything clearly. The professor approached me, paused for a moment, and then said:

"I have spoken with Ms. Johnes and thought everything over, but there is still so much I don't understand ..."

He was clearly wavering between two extremes—believing everything I had told him, or believing his personal knowledge and experience as a scientist. His discipline couldn't be broken so easily: a discipline derived from study, from knowledge based on experience itself, on the testimony of his own senses. To help him along, I said:

"One must believe a variety of things. Everything I have told you is the truth, plain and simple. I demonstrated it to you with Mr. Godínez's death."

"Ms. Johnes told me about what happened that night."

"Yes, I know. The mosquitoes informed me of your conversation. It must have been terrible for her, but it had to be done."

"And you maintain that everything you've said is true?"

"Yes," I answered him. "It's the truth, plain and simple. The mosquitoes will take over the entire world. They will make humans their slaves, in order to use them as their food source, as we have done with cattle and sheep ..."

"And you're taking part in this?" he asked me.

"Why shouldn't I?" I answered him. "I disdain mankind, and believe the mosquitoes will provide humans with a much better government."

There was a moment of quiet. The professor stared at me, as if realizing something, and hesitated. Finally, he said:

"I think you're completely mad—and that you're a dangerous madman. The Lacandon take you for a god; that laughable illusion of divinity has gone to your head and, using who knows what method, you killed Godínez to make us believe all these tall tales of yours. And the worst part is that some of my men are actually starting to believe you."

"They're right to believe me," I told him. "Maybe it will save their lives and land them a place in the organization of the new world."

"Well, I don't believe a word of it. I believe you went out of your way to murder Godínez because you're in love with Ms. Johnes."

"Lies!" I shouted.

"Yes," he continued, "that's why you did it. You murdered an innocent man and put the lives of my entire expedition at risk, and I've come to make good on my word. I've come to kill you."

His face was pale, as pale as his coat. His mustache was twitching.

"Now, don't go thinking that it will bring me any pleasure," he continued. "I've never killed a man before, and I revile homicide, but in this case I'm only doing what's right, so my conscience will be clean before God."

"You believe in God?" I asked him.

"Yes," he answered. "I believe in God, and that's why I'm going to kill you, because you're damaging the world, because you murdered Godínez, because you played a vile trick on these poor tribes and made them believe in some ridiculous divinity—by what means I have no clue, but I assure you they're perverse. I'm going to kill you not for personal revenge, not to avenge Godínez's death, but to save the world from such a deranged and dangerous man. I'm going to kill you, however much it repulses me, because I believe it to be my duty before God. Prepare to die."

And having warned me, he pulled a pistol out of one of his

blazer pockets. I was going to say something, but I didn't have time. The swarm of mosquitoes descended, blinding and suffocating him. He fired twice, but the mosquitoes had gone for his eyes and his bullets flew off, lost in the jungle. Then he dropped his pistol and tried to drive the mosquitoes away with his hands, clawing at his face with his nails in a desperate attempt to break free. He ran back and forth like a madman, while I picked up his pistol off the ground. I could hardly see him anymore, he was so covered by the swarm. Finally, he fell to the ground, a writhing black mass. A number of his men came running over, no doubt alerted by the two shots, but when they saw him thrashing in the brush among the mosquitoes, drenched in the blood pouring from the scratches he'd given himself and from his thousands of bites, they were petrified. I pointed at him with the gun and told them:

"Go back to your tents. The professor tried to kill me, and look what's happened: the mosquitoes are killing him."

They all returned obediently. The black mass stopped squirming and the mosquitoes dispersed. Professor Wassell was dead.

I moved his body with my foot to see if he was still alive, but no. Maybe he had suffocated; maybe he had died from horror and fear.

For a moment, I considered burying him, but I quickly saw all the hard work that would require, so I took him by his two feet, dragged him to the river, and threw him into the muddy waters, where the alligators would soon take note of him. I lived this entire scene in a sort of intellectual void, without thinking of a thing, my mind drawing a complete blank.

I returned to my hut and found Yellow Bird waiting at my door. He told me the white men had fled like madmen, leaving almost all their belongings behind.

I contacted Good Sun immediately. Those men were not to reach any civilized place or speak with anybody. Good Sun left, followed by vast squadrons, to stop them.

All through the night, I heard how the men screamed in the jungle. The mosquitoes had blinded them, and they were staggering around at random, falling and scrambling back up to their feet between the trees, splashing through the streams.

In her tent, Ms. Johnes was sleeping peacefully. Crazed with fright, the members of the expedition had forgotten her and left her all alone in my custody. I stood there for a long time, watching her sleep. Her face had a sweet, placid expression; her blonde hair fell to one side, almost reaching the ground.

By daybreak, the runaways had stopped screaming. Of Professor Wassell's expedition there survived only Ms. Johnes, asleep before me.

I was unmoved by the death of so many humans. Godínez had it coming to him for his betrayal of the professor. The professor, for trying to kill me—it's no crime to kill in self-defense. The others deserved to die for the cowardice they displayed in leaving Ms. Johnes behind. Their deaths, it is beyond question, were horrifying: blinded by mosquitoes, they staggered around shrieking through the jungle, cursing and praying at once, the men and that other woman alike, until they fell down, exhausted, into some puddle or against a tree trunk. Soon, the ants would find their way to them and begin stripping them of their flesh, leaving behind nothing but their clean, bare bones.

Yes, the mosquitoes' first battle had been fought and won.

XX

Good Sun found me early in the morning in Ms. Johnes's tent. She still hadn't woken up and I had been sitting there all night long, gazing at her white face and thinking bitter thoughts.

Good Sun spoke to me:

"The runaways have all died in the jungle, just as you'd warned them should they try to escape. Now the High Council has given the order for the woman to prepare herself to become their food source. She must report every day to the location we have indicated and allow suppliers to take her blood. This will happen every twenty-four hours until we have other humans to provide us blood."

"She can't go," I told him. "She's very sick—"

"And who are you to challenge the High Council's orders? They are already very displeased with you for all the humans who have died unnecessarily: they don't believe you have provided us a full picture of the situation. So, from now on, you must obey..."

"If it doesn't put his life in danger, we could use one of the Lacandon," I said slowly. Something inside me had broken, something that hurt, that made me feel as if I were drowning.

Good Sun laughed.

"Isn't that just like you humans? At first, you cared about your friends and begged us not to touch them. Now you want to sell them out to save this woman..."

"I don't think you understand," I told him. "This woman is sick and—"

"Oh, no," he interrupted me. "I understand perfectly well."

"So?" I asked him, full of hope.

"We mosquitoes know how to keep our word. We won't touch your Lacandon friends. The woman will be used as the High Council's food source."

"She can't! I'll give you deer blood—"

"The High Council has given its order, and your only concern is following it."

"I refuse," I told him.

"Come tomorrow, that woman will be where she's told to be, and she will let the suppliers take her blood. If you don't make sure of it, you'll both be dead."

Having said this, Good Sun disappeared, and I was left alone again with the sleeping woman and my torturous thoughts. At last, by midmorning, I thought I had found a way forward.

Florentino Kimbol was standing in the doorway.

"I'm going out," I told him. "Take care of the white woman until I get back. If she wakes up, tell her not to worry and give her food." Florentino looked at me with sadness. His deep, dark eyes followed me while I headed for my hut. In my own soul, too, were darkness and sorrow.

The jungle, the terrible, devastating, impulsive jungle, is like man's life. For years, it patiently nurses the majesty of its trees, and alongside that majesty, the very source of its own destruction. And so comes the day on which all that majesty falls back down to the earth and returns to dust and ash—and not by chance, but from that very devastating seed of destruction, that majesty created by the jungle itself. So is man, so was I, like the jungle: I destroyed my majesty; I, with the very hands with which I am writing these words, cast my monumental dreams to the ground. That's what I realized, sitting beside the white-faced woman. But now I understand it anew: it is no coincidence; I myself had carried the seed of this destruction in my own sick, tormented soil, and I had cultivated it, I myself, by falling in love with the children and the Lacandon whom I was now betraying. If all this had taken place before, when my soul knew nothing but hatred, my majesty would have lived on. But love and hate cannot coexist: the one destroys the other, and love, in the case of my soul, triumphed.

Slowly, I walked to my hut through the desolate clearing. I believe my feet, like Ms. Johnes's, were dragging themselves through the dust. But while I can say nothing certain of my feet, for I did not look at them, I do know for certain that my soul was dragging itself through the dust. When I arrived at the little beach, I looked for any mosquito I could talk to. Soon I heard the buzz of a supplier, and called to her. She flew over right away:

"Do you know who I am?" I asked her.

"Yes," she answered. "Who doesn't?"

"And you're aware of the things I've spoken of?"

"I am. All of us in the lower ranks are: our hopes are set on you."

"Gather your comrades and the troops," I told her, "as many as you can. The time has come for you to be free. But go in secret: I don't want the High Council to find out about our plans."

"The High Council knows everything," she said.

"There are many things that the High Council doesn't know," I replied. "It doesn't know, for example, what we're thinking, or what is going to happen next. All of you, together with the soldiers, are far greater in number than every High Council combined. These councils have done nothing but exploit you, and they live in leisure on your labor. The High Council has hidden the most important truth of all from you. It has hidden the existence of God."

"So, that's all real?"

"Yes, it's real. As real as you and me. God exists, God created everything—He is the great equalizer. The High Council never told you because it was afraid you would suddenly want to be their equals, which is exactly what is going to happen. Now, go and gather as many as you can and we'll see each other in three hours on this beach. I'll be waiting."

The supplier went buzzing off and I sat down to wait and think about what would happen next. Revolution was the only way to save Ms. Johnes, and if it succeeded, we would also save all of humanity from the slavery awaiting it. And then I *would* be the hero, the greatest man on earth, and my fame would be everlasting.

Little by little, the quiet jungle began to stir in the midday swelter. The shadows cast by every tree filled up with mosquitoes, silently waiting wherever they could. But regardless of the silence of their arrivals, the leaves trembled, sending out an uncanny murmur. Around three in the afternoon a captain appeared with a number of suppliers.

"Human," the captain said to me, "I believe we have gathered here everyone interested in our operation. We have more than six million soldiers, all of whom were raised for the coming war. In addition to that, we have some four million suppliers. Now, you must tell us how to begin."

"The first thing," I told them, "is to appoint leaders and for everyone to swear an oath to stay with our mission until the bitter end. For now, unless you have a better idea, let's appoint the highest-ranking captain among you and the supplier of your choice as your leaders."

A light rustling rose up from the leaves, and when it died down they elected a captain, with the discipline they'd honed over the centuries, introducing him to me as Audacious Strength. The suppliers chose as their leader the one I had sent to gather them all together, and I learned her name was Agility.

"Now," I told them, "we will all swear an oath to fight to the death for our objectives: for the equality of all mosquitoes; for the suppliers to have full say over the use of the blood they draw; for the soldiers who work and risk their lives in defense of the community to be duly compensated; for a new High Council to be elected by all, and for all mosquitoes to be eligible for election to the High Council."

"Approved," said Audacious Strength. "That is what we have been hoping for ever since the day you first spoke of God and equality."

"Now," I told them, "let's take our oath."

All present buzzed out their oaths. It turned into a Babel of sound and whirring. When all fell quiet, I said:

"Now we have to think about the best way to go about this."

"That's the hard part," said Audacious Strength. "We are not accustomed to thinking. We don't know how. We want you to think for us."

"Very well," I answered. "First and foremost, we have to work quickly to take the High Council by surprise. For that, we will need to know what forces the enemy has at its disposal. Do any of you know?"

"I know," one captain said. "In the treasury stockpiles, there are one hundred thousand soldiers armed with a variety of bacteria. There are around six hundred thousand more in the arsenal, plus about two million suppliers with their blood. The High Council security force consists of one million soldiers, of which more than half are with us now, but the rest are very well armed."

"Beyond that," one supplier said, "many of our comrades are abroad with the scouts, and we don't know whether they're with us or against us. And we mustn't forget the logicians, who number more than one hundred thousand and are able to fight, and the recordkeepers, whose quantity I don't know."

"All the logicians are with the High Council?" I asked with a pang, thinking of Good Sun.

"Yes," they answered. "They are all on the Council's side."

"From what I can tell," I told them, "we outnumber them and enjoy the element of surprise. I think we should begin the operations tonight, attacking all sites at once. I will stay here all night giving orders, guarded by a strong security force. Audacious Strength, you will lead one million soldiers to attack the High Council security force. Another captain will attack the treasury's security force with two hundred thousand soldiers and a million suppliers. Once you've taken it, you will destroy the greatest amount of larvae possible, because they are controlled by the accountants, who are not on our side ..."

I noticed everyone's shock when I said this; so I thought it might be a good idea to explain myself:

"If, for any reason, we should lose the treasury, the accountants will immediately raise millions of soldiers and wipe us out. That's why I want to destroy the larvae, out of an abundance of caution. And once the uprising has come to an end, the suppliers will no longer have to bring food to the High Council and can devote themselves exclusively to laying new eggs."

They were all satisfied with this explanation, and I proceeded with my orders.

"Another captain, with one million soldiers and two million suppliers—or more, if necessary—will attack the arsenal and hold it with extreme caution. The rest will stay behind as reserves, stationed in squadrons and ready to engage in combat, if necessary. Every captain will keep a special unit of suppliers on hand to run his messages. Is this clear?"

"Yes," they answered, "and we approve."

"There is only one thing left. In order to recognize each other and be sure our messages are authentic, we will use the word 'Freedom' as our password."

"Freedom," all buzzed in a cheer.

"Excellent," I said. "Now, everyone return to your work and don't buzz a word of this. One hour after sunset we will gather here and begin. I believe that, by morning, you will all be happy and free."

With a light rustling of leaves the crowd of mosquitoes vanished. I stood up, put away my flute, and headed for the caribal. Florentino Kimbol was sitting at the door of Ms. Johnes's tent, just as I had left him. Without greeting him, I walked into the tent. Ms. Johnes was still asleep in the same position as before, and I stopped to gaze at her for a long time, feeling Florentino's eyes nailed to my back. When the sun began to set, I left the tent and spoke to Florentino.

"One hour after sunset," I told him, "I want you to wake the woman up and take her to San Quintín as fast as you can. Stop for nothing, and if she is unable to walk, then carry her. But I beg you—make it to San Quintín with her tonight."

"It will be as you say," he replied.

But in his eyes was an even deeper sadness.

"If you don't take her away—if you don't take her far, far away from here, like I told you to—the evil spirits will descend upon the tribe. When I return at dawn, the woman cannot be here anymore. She absolutely must have left."

"Yes," he replied, "it will be as you say, O Kukulkan!"

"Take this money, and give it to her when you've made it to San Quintín. If she asks about me, don't tell her a thing."

Having said all this, I gave him some cash I'd found among Professor Wassell's things, and walked off toward the beach.

XXI

When Professor Wassell's watch, which I had also taken into my custody, showed 8:00 p.m., I dispatched the first squadrons to attack the High Council's den. They organized quickly and set off. I immediately set about preparing the squadrons that were to attack the treasury and arsenal. Given the discipline they had honed over so many centuries, they were easy to command and dispatch; I had finished in less than two hours, and the only ones left on the beach, dimly lit by the moon, were my security forces, and, hidden in the shadows of the trees, our reinforcements.

The first news arrived at ten thirty. The squadrons attacking the treasury security force had taken it and sent into retreat the few survivors, who had taken refuge in caves, and, as we had planned, our victorious troops were now busy destroying the larvae as fast as possible. Next I sent a strong group, of some five hundred thousand, to take the caves, lay siege on the mosquitoes in retreat, and if possible, annihilate them.

Around 11:00 p.m. I received news from the squadrons that had attacked the arsenal. They had stormed the germ-incubation pond, but as it turned out someone had tipped off the soldiers on guard; so the battle was harder fought, and although my troops ultimately emerged victorious, they had suffered a great number of casualties. I sent several squadrons, some three hundred thousand soldiers and a million suppliers, to hold the arsenal, ordering them to take no prisoners.

The squadrons that had me worried, however, were the ones

attacking the High Council security force. More than three hours had passed since their departure, and I still hadn't received any news. So, I sent a small group of suppliers to gather information. In the meantime, I decided it was time to attack the recordkeepers and take down the High Council once and for all.

One of the captains at my side informed me that the record-keepers generally gathered at night over a little pond downriver, and I sent all our reinforcements there with orders to kill every last one of them and to return as soon as possible.

Around 3:00 a.m. the suppliers I had sent off for an update on Audacious Strength's mission returned, but the reports were extremely confusing. Their captain was nowhere to be found. The battle seemed to have gone terribly, and the ground, the leaves on the trees, and the river were all blanketed with mosquito corpses. In certain areas there was still fighting, while others were perfectly silent. Some said victory was ours, while others said we had suffered a defeat.

Faced with such contradictory reports, I dispatched emissaries to the troops holding the arsenal, commanding all available squadrons to back up Audacious Strength. I sent the same message to the squadrons busy destroying the treasury, ordering them to leave that work to the suppliers and send all soldiers to the battle. I was left alone, with my security force reduced by half.

At last, some soldiers from Audacious Strength's fleet arrived, but they dismayed me even more. According to what they said, the High Council security force had doubled in size that night and the loyalist troops had been tipped off by the time the rebels arrived. Audacious Strength attacked courageously, hoping to come away victorious for his greater number of soldiers, but endless new enemy forces kept streaming out of the caves. Another one of the mosquitoes who returned after watching his squadron get devastated told me that the High Council probably kept a large secret reserve of reinforcements in the caves near its residence, and that these had lent a hand.

I rallied them the best I could, assuring them that we had sent our own reinforcements and had emerged victorious from our other two missions; but I was still midspeech when a number of suppliers arrived to say they had come from the treasury and that, as soon as my troops had left to help Audacious Strength, countless loyalist soldiers came from out of nowhere and massacred them, killing them all.

"Had they already destroyed the larvae?" I asked them.

"Almost."

"At least we came out on top there," I told them. "The High Council can't replace its troops, so they're in the same situation as us. Go," I told one of them, "and find the squadrons I sent to kill the recordkeepers and tell them to report to the High Council to back up Audacious Strength."

"There's no use," said a badly injured trooper who had just arrived from the battle. "Audacious Strength has been taken captive by the High Council, and our squadrons have been destroyed."

"It doesn't matter," I told him. "The other squadrons will go and fight until the end. Only a small security detail will stay behind with me."

They all set out on the path in silence. A deep sadness had taken hold of us, the sadness of defeat, which contrasted starkly with the deep blue sky and the bright moonlight. I don't know why I remembered my childhood then—those days I spent dreaming of great battles, imagining that defeats always took place under cloudy skies, as on a stamp I had once seen of Napoleon in retreat from Waterloo. That clear moonlit sky, without a cloud in it, disturbed me even more than the defeat itself.

A messenger brought me the news that the High Council security force, now more than three million soldiers strong, was attacking and slowly beating our own troops back through the jungle. The squadrons I had sent to take out the recordkeepers hadn't succeeded in their mission, and returning in scattered groups, flew off to join the fight against the High Council security force.

I gave no more orders: it was pointless. The murmur of combat was slowly approaching through the jungle. My troops were retreating to the beach, ragged and defeated. Alone, I sat down on the ground and waited. My security detail, perched around me on the sand, didn't make a sound. Suddenly, I couldn't handle their silence anymore, and I sent them off to the fight. They all rose and flew off in silence, with the air of creatures who know they are about to die.

I didn't want to meditate on the reasons behind my defeat. Our plan had failed, millions of mosquitoes had died, I myself was almost certainly going to die, but the important thing had been achieved: Ms. Johnes, during the course of the battle, which I had prolonged as long as possible, had made it safely to San Quintín and civilization. Once the battle had ended and the mosquitoes tried to hunt her down, it would be too late.

The murmur of combat drew closer and closer to the beach. I could already clearly hear the shouting of my partisans, their cries of "Freedom!" and those of the High Council, who called out to each other with "Ideal!"—though I never did understand why they used this unusual password.

My watch, or Professor Wassell's, rather, said it was three in the morning when the first combatants arrived on the beach. They clashed one-on-one, braiding their legs together; but because the High Council loyalists outnumbered us, two or three of them often attacked a single mosquito of mine in tandem and killed him. And as soon as the victors had freed themselves up, they immediately sprang upon their nearest enemy and repeated the operation. And so some advanced while others got driven back, until the battle was being fought over the lake. Corpses were raining down, and soon the water was blanketed with them, just like the sand on the beach.

I stood up and watched the scene in silence. There was nobody left I could give orders to: I was a commander without a general staff, marooned. A group of enemies surrounded me; none of them came close, but they hemmed me in on all sides like a levitating wall. It was the same swarm I had seen over Professor Wassell's head before it killed him—and suddenly I felt afraid, terribly afraid, faced with the horrific death that awaited me. As the only thing left for me to do, I took out my flute and buzzed orders to my troops:

"Fly away! Fly away! We have lost the battle."

A captain among the mosquitoes surrounding me said:

"Why do you want them to flee, human? They will die anyway, and their kind will go extinct. You led them into evil, into point-less death—mosquitoes can't survive without the High Council."

I sat down again to wait on the sand. The swarm around me had grown increasingly dense, increasingly quiet and terrifying. The murmur of combat withdrew over the lake and, stranded in enemy territory, I was alone, terribly alone with my fear. I tried to think about Ms. Johnes, safe now in San Quintín, but her image made me sad, because I knew I would never lay eyes on her again. I didn't want to think about anything, but ideas kept attacking me just to hurt me—thoughts of the power I had forfeited, my useless life, Ms. Johnes ...

A buzzing voice snapped me out of it:

"Human," it said, "the High Council awaits you. It will be your judge, so start walking. You know where to go."

I stood up and walked across the beach, surrounded by the swarm, which moved along with me without ever drawing nearer or moving further away. I thought about throwing myself into the water and swimming away from them, but where could I go? They could drown me in the water even more easily than they could kill me on land.

When I arrived at the place where I had spoken with the Su-preme Council that very first time, I saw the black mass at the foot of the giant mahogany tree. I stopped before it, and a voice buzzed to me:

"What do you have to say for yourself, human?"

"Nothing," I answered. "Kill me or do with me as you like. You have defeated me in battle—"

"We aren't interested in your pretty phrases," they told me. "You betrayed the High Council and broke your word: you deserve to die."

"Yes, but I want to tell you—"

"We aren't interested in your reasons, either. You betrayed us, and you are going to die like all the mosquitoes you persuaded into evil. The damage you have caused is grave and one hundred years will pass before we have overcome it—"

"I'm glad to hear it," I interrupted him. "What I want to tell you is—"

"Be quiet. By this time tomorrow, wherever you are, you will be dead. We know how to find you. Now, you may go."

I wanted to answer, but the black mass had already dispersed. I had already known they were going to sentence me to death, but I was hoping for another kind of trial: a trial with fine phrases, heroic phrases like the ones I had dreamt of in my youth. This trial, in which I wasn't even allowed to speak, filled me with bitterness. The only thought that brought me any comfort was that Ms. Johnes had escaped, and I wanted to shout it in their faces so they'd see that their victory wasn't complete. And I did shout it out at them, but the jungle's hush was my only answer.

I walked slowly back to my hut, wondering how to spend that day, the last day of my life. That's when I decided to write all of this down, so my name could live on forever.

Day was breaking, with the usual commotion of birds and animals rustling among the leaves. I felt alone, so utterly alone. But I saw a man squatting at my door with a small object in his hand, something like a clay pot. I walked over and saw it was Florentino Kimbol.

"What are you doing here?" I asked him. "I told you to take—"

"Don't be angry with me, O Kukulkan! I have disobeyed you,

but I know my disobedience will not upset you and that you will look upon me with loving eyes, the very same eyes that looked upon my people and—"

"Where is the woman?" I asked, cutting him off.

"Let me tell you, O Kukulkan! O Quetzalcóatl, as the Nahuas have named you! O great white bird! You, the bearded, the strong, the good!"

And as he said this, he fell to his knees before me and offered me a clay pot draped in a white cloth, which he lifted in his hands.

"I have thought deep within, and I have said: The god suffers in his heart because the blonde woman's heart does not belong to him. And he has told me: Florentino Kimbol, bring the blonde woman to San Quintín. But I know the man's heart will follow the woman, though he be a god, because he desires creation. And I have told myself: The god Kukulkan must not leave us; the task falls on you to keep him among us. And I have taken a dagger and removed the woman's heart, and I have brought it to you, so that your heart may rejoice."

Having said this, he uncovered the clay pot, and I saw a russet heart drying inside it.

I said nothing, accepted the clay pot, walked to her tent, took her corpse in my arms, and returned to my hut with both her body and heart.

Prostrating himself before the rising sun, Florentino Kimbol was praying in the doorway and weeping.

"O Kukulkan! Accept this blood I have offered you. I know the gods love blood, and that is why I have offered it to you—in order to please you, for you are a powerful god."

Unable to bear his clamoring any longer, I asked him to leave and closed my door.

XXII

And here I am, still writing, in my hut. Night has fallen and I have lit Professor Wassell's lamp. Ms. Johnes's body lies in the stillness of the night, and on the table before me sits the little clay pot with her dry and blackening heart, from which I have to shoo the flies away every so often.

This is the heart of a woman, I tell myself, this darkling hunk of flesh is the heart of a woman I once saw so full of life. And that, upon my bed—with a face as white as wax and blonde hair cascading all the way to the floor, with that horrible red stain upon its breast—is a woman. In the heat of the afternoon, her rigid flesh has begun to rot; a harsh and sour smell wafts from it and burns my throat.

But I too am going to die. I think of God, I think of Him, and I try to do so with the faith of my grandmother, the one who taught me Father Ripalda's catechism, sitting in her wide shady corridor beside her potted plants. But God has slipped out of my hands. Was it my pride? Someone, maybe a priest, once told me you have to be humble if you want to find God.

Now, with my dreams undone, sitting beside this corpse, I understand so much. Florentino Kimbol has gone deep into the jungle where he will die because his god looked upon him with scornful eyes. Maybe the last act of my life should be to go console him, but I feel a terrible weariness in my legs, the weariness that signals the onset of death.

Death. I brought death into my crazed dreams of power. But I

won't have to die. I'll live on in the pages I've written; I'll live forever, and my name won't be lost like the names of the mosquitoes
who followed me in my rebellion. That's why I wrote it clearly on
the first page of this notebook and every other—the one with my
Dictionary of the Mosquil Language, and the other with its gram-
mar. My name is there, and will live on through the centuries.

But my body? This body that my grandmother called poorly
made, and which I've loved for nearly fifty years? This body for
which I sought power, glory, strength? Tomorrow it will be like
Ms. Johnes's, but as I think of this, anxiety clutches my throat and
I feel like screaming into the night, screaming at the heart of the
jungle. This isn't fair—it's impossible. I, the center of a world, of
my world—I, who have achieved so much, achieved more than
any other man—I . . . I can't, I mustn't die.

Maybe you also need strength to die. When I started writing
these memoirs I felt strong and serene, but now, sitting beside Ms.
Johnes's corpse—so white, so cold, so vacant of emotion—I feel
afraid, terrified and afraid.

In the corner of my hut sit Professor Wassell's crates of liquor . . .

Oh, I feel better now. I'm not afraid anymore, my hands no longer
tremble as I write: It is I, the most powerful man alive! The immortal—immortal because God created me in His likeness. But
how can I stand before God? How can I present these dreams
of mine, and that absurd corpse laid out on my bed, and that
desiccated heart in the clay pot, which are my dreams' inevitable
conclusions?

I am sad—this liquor is sad, and its droplets trickle down
slowly inside me and carry sorrow down every pathway of my
body. I am sad and speaking of and looking upon myself with bitterness, copying myself out on paper, so that my name, the one I
have inscribed on the first page of every notebook, my immortal
name, will never be lost. I am sad—how I'd like to kneel alone in

the jungle and say something, anything, maybe those words my grandmother once taught me, those words I recited with such faith as a boy. But my tongue no longer responds to those words, and my knees quake whenever I try to stand. The smell of the corpse only grows sourer, its face more hollow, but I feel empty and I'm not afraid of death. I laugh in death's face!

I take Ms. Johnes's body in my arms. How funny to think now ... I never even knew her first name! Maybe it was Maria. And we will go together, through the jungle—yes, I'll carry her. She without a heart, and I with my heart mended and broken once more. She with her face grown thin and her heavy, sour smell. Oh, how I'd like to kneel beside her, and kiss her hand, and tell her I'm so very sorry ...

Outside my hut, the jungle calls to me. And I will go into her, with this corpse in my arms, in search of my death.

Epilogue

Colonel Pérez slammed the notebook shut and asked Yellow Bird to hand over the other notebooks and the first pages that were missing from the one he had read. Yellow Bird answered:

"Kukulkan, the white, the good, taught us to make paper boats and cast them into the river, so the waters might carry away the evil spirits. We have taken twenty-four sheets every day since Kukulkan went away from us, leaving us his dry heart in a clay pot. Soon all the sheets of paper will have sailed away, and then Kukulkan, the Wise Owl, will speak to us and tell us his wishes."

"I'll have to confiscate this notebook," said the colonel. "What was the man's name?"

"He was Kukulkan, the wise, the white, the good, the great, the bearded, the one the Nahuas call Quetzalcóatl, who returned to us so our peoples could rule the earth once again."

"What was his name, I said," demanded the colonel, in no mood for fooling around.

"We called him the Wise Owl, but we know he was Kukulkan, the good, the—"

"Enough!" the colonel interrupted, unwilling, under any circumstances, to hear the litany that awaited him again. "I'll be taking this notebook and leaving this instant. It'll rain before long, and I have no intention of getting stuck here."

The sergeant wrapped the notebooks in a waterproof cloth. The colonel was in one hell of a mood, having walked for seven days through that infernal jungle in search of an expedition of idiotic scientists who had ventured so deep they couldn't find their way out, only to wrap up his trip by finding a grave—which, according to the tribes, belonged to one of those very scientists— and the diaries or memoirs of some deadbeat lunatic whose real name he wasn't able to include in his police report because no one actually knew it. How was he, in good faith, supposed to write in official documents that all the members of this internationally renowned expedition had been killed by mosquitoes acting on the orders of Kukulkan, or the Wise Owl?

"Let's go," the colonel said.

The carriers threw what was left of Professor Wassell's impedimenta over their shoulders, and the detachment disappeared into the jungle.

And Yellow Bird, along with his entire tribe, wept:

"O Kukulkan, the wise and good! Men who resemble you have come and taken away the paper where you engraved the symbols that drive away the evil spirits. But with the white and fair-haired woman you have left us—and you have taken Florentino Kimbol with you as your servant. Come back to us, O bird of white feathers, O Kukulkan!"